Mrs. Sartoris

MRS. SARTORIS

■ ■ ■

Elke Schmitter

TRANSLATED FROM THE GERMAN
BY CAROL BROWN JANEWAY

 ALFRED A. KNOPF   NEW YORK   2003

THIS IS A BORZOI BOOK
PUBLISHED BY ALFRED A. KNOPF

www.aaknopf.com

Originally published in Germany as *Frau Sartoris*
by Berlin Verlag, Berlin, in 2000. Copyright © 2000 by
Berlin Verlag, Berlin.
Knopf, Borzoi Books, and the colophon are registered trademarks
of Random House, Inc.

Library of Congress Cataloging-in-Publication Data

Schmitter, Elke, [date]
[Frau Sartoris. English]
Mrs. Sartoris / by Elke Schmitter; translated from the German by
Carol Brown Janeway.
p. cm.
—1st American ed.
ISBN 0-375-41186-0
I. Janeway, Carol Brown.   II. Title.
PT2680.M569F7313 2003
833'.92—dc21   2002043324

Manufactured in the United States of America
First American Edition

The statement is pointless
The finger is speechless

—RONALD D. LAING, *Knots*

I see myself as a piece on the chessboard, and the opponent is saying, "This piece may not be moved."

—SØREN KIERKEGAARD, *Either/Or*

MRS. SARTORIS

The street was empty. It was drizzling, as it often did in this region, and twilight was giving way to darkness—so you can't say that the visibility was good. Perhaps that's why I was so late in spotting him, but it was also probably because I was deep in thought. I'm often deep in thought. Not that anything comes of it.

■ ■ ■

I was on the way home. I had been shopping in the town and had met Renate, who had come over to L. for the afternoon. We had a drink, really just one—two at the most. I knew I would be driving, and besides, Ernst checks my breath. Sometimes he does it for some reason that may have nothing to do with me. He comes out to meet me before I reach the front door, to relieve me of the shopping bags or some other excuse. He strokes my cheek with a kiss, inhaling deeply along the way. He doesn't know I figured it out long ago, because he prides himself on using his knowledge discreetly. This means he doesn't reproach me immediately. He bides his time, even if it's only for a minute—however long it takes me to make an excuse and get through the door. Or skip the excuse, if we're alone.

So I didn't drink a lot. Maybe one, two sherries. If you're a wine drinker, the only thing they serve in Hirmer's Café is a Moselle, because Hirmer Senior, when he opened the place more than ninety years ago, was a Moselle fanatic, which was quite common back then. It's a big wine, and too sweet for us these days, and sweet isn't even the right word. There's something too full-bodied about it, it's too heavy to drink with anything except meat in aspic, and they no longer serve meat in aspic at Hirmer's either. So when we're there, Renate and I drink sherry. It tastes okay going down, and it's cheap compared with Campari or other respectable drinks. We can hardly drink schnapps, because we're in L. after all, and I live here, and when a lady lives here, if she ever feels like having a drink for no reason and she's not part of some group, she orders sherry.

The first time I saw her was in Dr. Lehmkuhl's waiting room. Dr. Lehmkuhl's grandfather still had a big farm outside town, his father had been the first interim mayor after the war, and he himself had a major reputation as a neurologist. I was there because my nerves were in a state—or more precisely, because Irmi and Ernst had noticed. I set off in the car to buy bread and soap powder and came back with cigarettes, which Ernst gave up ten years ago. I forgot my godchildren's birthdays and pulled up the marigolds I'd sowed in the garden myself, because I mistook the stalks for weeds. Twice I suffered every housewife's nightmare of leaving the burner of the stove on with an empty pot on top. There are apparently electric stoves you can get now that switch themselves off before the pot melts and there's a catastrophe. But we had an old one, because that's what Irmi manages best. She has her head together as well.

The two of them decided something was the matter with me. And they were right. That I slept badly at night and sometimes dozed off in the early evening on the sofa was nothing new. I could even make Ernst believe it had always been like that. He didn't know that I often woke up at one-thirty in the night and lay awake till morning, doggedly watching the peregrinations of the hands round the face of the alarm clock. The hands glow in the dark; the clock was a honeymoon present from Irmi. Things like that were incredibly modern back then and also much better made. The clock will outlive us all.

But the state of my nerves was something new to them. Both of them claimed they were worried about me, and I actually believed it of Irmi. Their conversations would sometimes break off when I came into the living room, or Irmi would lower her voice when she was talking to Ernst in her room. Eventually their verdict was unanimous: I was going to harm myself. They couldn't very well involve Daniela; she was already quite independent for her age and didn't let herself be told much anyway—unless she wanted to get permission to spend the night at a friend's house.

So an appointment was made with Dr. Lehmkuhl, and I went—I didn't even put up a fight.

When it came right down to it, I didn't care one way or the other, and the thought of someone taking care of me was an appealing one. There was a woman sitting in the waiting room who was around my age, clothes a little loud, expensive jewelry on both wrists, and the kind of subtle tan that signals regular skin care and sessions with a sunlamp. I didn't know her by sight, which in a town like L. is quite a surprise. Sooner or later you meet someone like that at the theater, or at a coffee morning or one of Ernst's club evenings. She thumbed through magazines, glancing up periodically at the clock, and then sighed so heavily that it would almost have been impolite not to react. We exchanged a glance, and she asked in a deep, very attractive voice if one always had to wait so long here. I said this was my first visit too, and that's how we fell into conversation. Although she didn't know anyone in town, she didn't seem to be lonely or afflicted in any way, on the contrary she radiated energy. When the nurse finally came into the waiting room to make apologies for Dr. Lehmkuhl—he had been called out on an emergency and unfortunately would not be back at the practice before the end of the day—she collected her things abruptly, put a wonderful lightweight pale summer coat over her arm, and invited me to a cup of coffee: the afternoon was wasted anyway, so why didn't we make something out of it? And so we did. When I came home after dinner, Irmi and Ernst stared at me in amazement. They were probably asking themselves if Dr. Lehmkuhl had dispensed neat alcohol by way of a prelude to his treatment. But it wasn't Dr. Lehmkuhl, it was my friend Renate. And it wasn't neat alcohol, it was a very good red wine. Good for the blood vessels, at least.

Further appointments were made, of course. I liked Dr. Lehmkuhl right away. A sinewy man, obviously a tennis player; he emanated self-control and rigor, which impressed me. I immediately told him more about myself than Irmi and Ernst will ever know; he listened patiently and without emotion, but in such a way that I knew I was understood. He did some tests—tapping the knee-caps, tickling the soles of the feet, etc.—with care but a lack of enthusiasm that conveyed a belief, which I shared, that there was nothing to be learned from them. He asked me about drinking—perhaps Ernst had put him onto this—and I lied to him with an equanimity born of long practice. Much later, I poured him red wine, straight up. It was fun to watch him shake his head and to know that his helplessness was tinged with fellow-feeling. He had certainly noticed my talent for being able, at will, to seem healthy or sick, energetic or frail, aggressive or sweet, as circumstances required, and yet he also sensed that I didn't want to play games with him. I didn't want to lose his attention, and that involved being honest with him—up to a point.

He gave me pills. He did it unwillingly, as he told me, but because I refused to switch to one of his colleagues who was a psychotherapist—I was perfectly aware why this would be a bad idea—it seemed to him the only way to help me for the moment. I took the first dose in his office, and I can still remember the feeling of armorplated protection I had when I got home. I was more alert than usual; I emptied the ashtrays, said good night to Daniela in her room, and left the car key in the exact place where Ernst always wanted it left. I was enjoying myself along the way, watching myself doing all this and congratulating myself the way we used to congratulate the poodle when he came to us carrying his bowl in his mouth. My imperturbability seemed strange even to me, and when Ernst asked me how I felt, I said: the same way our car feels right after it's been inspected. For him, my visit to the doctor had its desired effect: I was functioning again. If only for that first evening.

Because I didn't get the prescription filled. I decided to pull myself together, and it went reasonably well. I wanted to go back to Dr. Lehmkuhl, but I wanted to get through the days without some official inspection sticker saying I was okay. There were times when I dealt with the whole daily round—getting my child to kindergarten and the school, making two meals a day and serving them at set times, shopping, doing the garden, organizing children's birthdays, appearing at club evenings, doing holidays, doing bookkeeping and finances, hairdresser's appointments and obedience school for the dog, doing Easters and Christmases and on and on—I dealt with the whole thing as if it went without saying. And that wasn't really the problem anyway.

I don't know when it got lost. The certainty, the strength, the concentration that was automatically there for what is known as everyday life. I can still see myself sitting on the sofa with Ernst, and Irmi in the big armchair that we had had reupholstered. We would eat crackers and salted nuts, drink beer or wine, even schnapps later in the evening. I can see Peter Frankenfeld and Dieter Thomas Heck, Hans Rosenthal, and Hans Joachim Kulenkampff as clearly as if they were my brothers-in-law. Carrell who couldn't pronounce his *r*'s, Kulenkampff's broad grin. Whenever there was ballet on television, Ernst always said, "Our girls aren't so bad either," and Irmi or I would agree with him. We'd watch those muscular thighs working away as they swung forward and backward, left and right, and I would look down surreptitiously at my legs—those were the days when we wore gabardine trousers in dark colors, brown or blue, very close-fitting— and think about a diet. Irmi and I tried them all, for Ernst's sake too, because he claimed he was battling his paunch. But no matter what we cooked in the evenings— steamed vegetables, lean fish, even fillet steak and salad— none of it changed a thing. Ernst blamed it on his digestion, but when it came down to it, all three of us knew that the evening beers and schnapps and nuts and chips and breadsticks and double-thick sandwiches were having their effect. And Irmi didn't want it any other way. "Isn't this cozy!" she always said as she poured another little glass of wine, took the bowl of peanut flips, and beamed at us. Ernst's paunch didn't bother her—he was a grown

man, after all!—and she attributed my spreading waist-
line to having given birth. Daniela was a heavy baby, she
said from time to time. Both of us knew this was a lie:
Daniela was made of feathers, light as a butterfly, with
red-gold down for hair, eyes that were almost transparent, more of a delicate moth than a baby.

She had inherited nothing from either of us. I can
still feel the shock I felt the first time I saw her—she
seemed absolutely foreign to me, and after some hesitation I asked the nurse whether it was possible there had
been a mix-up. She looked at me, disconcerted, and would
have launched into a hymn to mother love but the sister
was already in the room. What are you thinking of, Mrs.
Sartoris! she declaimed in vigorous horror, you were the
only woman to be delivered this morning, and besides,
all the babies get a tag on their ankle, and you can see,
it's all on there: time of birth, weight at birth, length, body
temperature, name of doctor in charge; mix-ups are
impossible. Enjoy your little baby girl, I haven't seen
such a beautiful baby for . . . and so on and so on. I was
far too exhausted to contradict her, and besides I wanted
to make my peace with this remarkable creature lying in
a portable crib next to my bed. Yet as far as I still knew,
Ernst's hair was mouse brown, and my own mop of curls
was dark blond, as was Irmi's hair, and this daughter of
mine, my first and last, had red-gold down on her head
and was so delicate she could disappear at any moment,
whereas the rest of us were tall and quite well built.
Later a priest arrived too, and said some nice words of

praise for me and the baby. Then came Ernst and Irmi with carnations and women's magazines, then came the tasks that ran from day to night and back to day again, the fennel tea, the walking to and fro with her, the hopeless attempts to stop her crying, and Irmi's inexhaustible interventions. Some years ago, when we were having a fight, Ernst said the only reason I had accepted him when he proposed was Irmi. I didn't tell him the truth—not then, not later—but as a supposition it's not entirely wrong. When we got engaged, Irmi had just turned fifty, and she dazzled me. She was a war widow, her only son had had one lower leg blown away in battle, her income could even be described as wretched—but she always looked as if she'd won the lottery and was just waiting for people she could share it with. The first time she saw me—it was an overcast Sunday afternoon in April, warm and sticky, as it often is around here—she immediately embraced me and led us into the parlor for coffee as if I were the daughter of a queen. Ernst told me you are beautiful, she said as she cut into the cake, but he didn't tell me just how beautiful you are!

That afternoon wasn't the decisive one. I had gone more or less out of boredom; the time I'd spent in the sanatorium had shriveled me up. I wanted to be surrounded by people and activity, and anything that achieved this was fine by me. The idea that Ernst the quintessential club man wanted to introduce me to his mother struck me as quite comic, but there weren't many distractions back then, and an afternoon of pound cake and local gossip was definitely more entertaining than sitting around at my parents' house. We opened a bottle of Rhine wine and played cards until late in the dark; I hadn't laughed so much for months. Irmi positively enjoyed losing; she piled the pennies on my side of the table and said these are for the bridal shoes and never once looked at Ernst, and that really pleased me. As we were walking home—it went without saying in those days that a man would accompany his young lady back home, even if that meant the other end of town—I was raving to Ernst about his mother, while he remained monosyllabic. Perhaps he had had all too much experience as an awkward young man, already ten years an invalid, of being outshone by his mother in her gaiety and the good mood she created around her. It was almost as if he regretted that we'd spent a Sunday afternoon (when the local football team was playing) in our own little group with his mother on the edge of town, away from his regular friends, with the surprising result that his mother and I—the girl who above all didn't want to be anyone's bride—came together in a friendly pact and made the tiniest bit of fun of him.

He did not find himself the slightest bit funny. He cared a great deal about his appearance, bought his suits at Moll's, and polished his shoes to a high gloss. When he walked, he barely dragged the leg with the prosthesis at all, and if you hadn't known better, you would have assumed that the faint hesitation in his left foot was merely a physical quirk. He was well built, with a tendency to corpulence detectable only in his chin. His father had been stocky, as you could see from the photograph on the sideboard—in uniform, looking vaguely but firmly away at a half-right angle from the viewer, a kind of standard expression back then. You sensed rather than saw the girth below the chest. Ernst didn't have much to tell about him, and even Irmi kept silent for a long time about her marriage.

Without hesitation I was immediately ready to attribute all Ernst's annoying characteristics—including his ridiculous name—to his father. For example, Irmi was always proper and took herself seriously, as was the expression back then, but Ernst's displays of pedantry must have come from Heinz-Günther. The way on every trip he kept reaching into his wallet to check the tickets, his mania for placing his glasses on the top right-hand corner of the TV guide, his throat-clearing every time we sat down to eat—all these tics, which made him seem so much older than he was, must have come from his father. He could check himself in the mirror three or four times to be sure his hair was parted straight before we set off for a club event. He laid out the amount of money he was prepared to spend in the course of an evening, then sorted it back into his wallet, having put the surplus bills into a tin in the sideboard. He never helped me on with my coat without saying "May I please?" which went back to some joke in his youth which he had totally forgotten, along with its punch line, but which had this one utterly pointless detail in it that stuck with him and that he never wearied of repeating. And finally there was this way he had of picking up things—a menu, an ashtray, a garden spade—as if he doubted their utility or their very substance. He hesitated to take hold of them properly and instead he turned them a little, checking each thing's fit, as if the world were some kind of prosthetic device that would go kaput if you grabbed onto it too hard. He couldn't hold me properly either. I cannot remember our first kiss, but I still know the feeling of his hand reaching under my blouse for the first time, his fingers grasping as carefully as they had when they were searching for his napkin at dinner shortly before.

All pleasures back then were harmless. What was there to do in L.?! Saturday afternoons, bowling, followed by a "happy circle" of the club. I was too exhausted to wonder about this, I just went along. Twenty or thirty of you sat at a long table, very occasionally at several tables, and talked about something. Politics was taboo, so was the past, and the future was confined to two-room apartments in town, an allotment on the outskirts, and your father's workshop. There were some employees in the group—Freddy and Thomas, for example—and you could recognize them by the fact that they paid more attention to their appearance and were carefully polite. Ernst fitted right in. He was also much loved. Almost nobody had a TV set at home, the only movie house in L. didn't change its programs more than once every few weeks—so people were drawn to anyone with something approaching talent. And to some degree Ernst had talent.

His mother had taught him to play the lute. Irmi was very musical; whenever someone started singing a folk song or a popular hit, she would slip spontaneously into singing harmony in a beautiful, soft alto voice. Her first love was operetta, and in the fifties and sixties the radio was full of it. *The Gypsy Baron, The Cousin from Nowhere, The Czardas Princess,* etc. She knew the most famous arias by heart, complete with libretto, and accompanied herself on the lute. She did duets with Ernst, the two of them sang to each other, and it was beautifully done and quite unself-conscious; however, on club evenings Ernst performed solo. On these occasions he also sang operetta favorites, but deliberately chose the ones with silly words, which allowed him to roll his eyes and make extravagant gestures. He acted out the Italian in love, the hot-blooded Hungarian, and the Cousin from Nowhere by chortling, snorting, cooing, and snapping his fingers; it was all absolutely perfect, and yet the result was that everything became a joke: the music, the text, Ernst, even the audience. You've become so serious! my mother often said, and pushed me, whenever I was hesitating about whether I wanted to go on one of these evenings with Ernst: Go, it'll do you good, these young people are full of energy and it's time you enjoyed yourself again!

I would have to wait a long time for that to happen. I no longer knew the last time I had laughed, but I did

know the last time I had been happy: it was when I slit
open the last letter from Philip and ran with it into my
room.

He wrote to me a lot. Not just because we couldn't
see each other every day, but also because letters allowed
him to talk about himself. He didn't find it easy in person, and he turned aside any direct questions I asked. I
sensed that things hadn't been easy for him, that he had
had a difficult childhood and the future looked pretty
confusing.

It was Ulrike who had introduced us. She was younger
than me, and the future heir of Dr. Hermann, Wholesale
and Retail Machine Parts and Tools, where my father
worked. Not exactly a friend. We knew each other because
she always accompanied her father on Christmas Eve
when he went round delivering the Christmas bonuses to
all the employees in person, along with a box of candy
and greetings from his wife. I don't know if he also went
to all the workmen, it wasn't something that occurred to
me back then—but it wasn't something that could have
been done in a day. So Ulrike always came along; even as
a little girl, she had a funny way about her, and later she
came to enjoy her role—like a little Eastern princess, gra-
ciously dispensing her gifts to the poor. You said your
thank-you's and offered them coffee, and in the first
years she sat on her father's lap, drank a glass of apple
juice, and stared openly all around the room. Later she
too had a cup of coffee, made herself comfortable on the
sofa, and attempted, rather precociously, to make con-

versation. She was well on her way to becoming the queen of the castle, and nobody would have believed that twenty years later, after two unhappy marriages and the sale of her father's company, she would be found dead in a hotel room in F.

We weren't friends, but we did know each other, and because I was two years older, she looked up to me a little when she was young. She admired the dresses my mother made from sketches I'd done—a strawberry-pink summer dress with a big soft collar and mother-of-pearl buttons, a winter suit of bouclé wool with a short jacket and a long, narrow skirt, a coat of bottle-green chintz with a deep inverted pleat at the back. She was quite pretty as a girl, but totally lacking in charm, and she knew it, and it made her unhappy. One evening she drove to our house with her father's chauffeur: a girl had dropped out of her dancing class; they were practicing some difficult steps right then, and the boys didn't want to miss out on anything. She knew that I could dance. I was a bit embarrassed and also offended to be invited to this dance like an employee being permitted to make herself particularly useful, but my pleasure in the cha-cha won out. I still remember myself quite exactly, standing in front of the wardrobe and choosing what to wear—a cream-colored dress with a wide skirt that would swing as I turned.

We were introduced to each other in front of the portico. The Blumenthal House, the leading address in town for such social events, had a stretch of garden in front that was like a park; it was quite hot, and most of the young people were standing around on the lawn under the trees, chatting and laughing. My own dancing class had met in a community hall; the Blumenthal House was quite out of the question, far too expensive and also not really appropriate. I was familiar with the Art Deco reception rooms and their castlelike size from guided tours; I even knew where the toilets were. This literally gave me confidence. I didn't understand his name. I have always had trouble—and it's never gotten any better—taking in a face and a name at one and the same time. I always settle for the face, as I did then, in the park, in the dusk. I looked into dark brown eyes with lashes as long as a girl's; there was something warm in his gaze that attracted me, and something yearning that left me helpless. Ulrike's friend was blond, with a white handkerchief in his jacket pocket, a cigarette holder, and pale eyes that were often half shut. He inspected me briefly, complimented Ulrike on her good taste, and passed me on with a nonchalant gesture to his companion, the one whose name I hadn't grasped. I was enraged by his snottiness, but Ulrike made me feel awkward: she was hanging on his arm as if drunk with happiness, laughing idiotically for no discernible reason; I didn't want my bad temper to trouble her, and perhaps there was something that had escaped my notice. So we looked at each other again, the companion and I; he sensed my embarrassment and I sensed his vulnerability. Where do you

learn how to behave with a young girl who is being sub-
jected to careless bad manners and whom you have only
just met?

I simply took his arm and we strolled around the
pebbled pathways. Actually what I was doing was more
like marching, but the paths were wide enough, and the
pebbles noisy enough for us not to have to make conversation. And I gradually calmed down. The trees rustled
above our heads; I felt pretty in my dress, with its high
collar that made you aware of your neck muscles, so that
you held your head erect. The wide bell-shaped skirt put
a swing in my stride and made it confident. In the meantime he had taken my arm; his hand exerted no pressure,
it was just warm and light. We looked neither at each
other nor at anyone else, so nobody said hello to him
and nothing interrupted our rhythm; I don't know how
many circuits we made.

When the groups finally broke up and everyone
headed for the house, he stopped for a moment, let go of
my arm, bowed, glanced at me for a second, and said a
very formal "thank you." Our dance was like a dream.
He led comfortably, but not insistently, so that I, who
liked to lead myself, was able to rely on him completely.
We moved according to the rules, which meant no looking at each other—I kept my eyes over his shoulder and
he steered us carefully through the other couples. It
began with a slow waltz; my hand rested lightly on his
upper arm; I felt the smooth, well-tailored cloth; a deli-

cate citrus scent enveloped him all evening. Next came a classic fox-trot, then the teaching part began with a rumba.

It was always my favorite dance. You were allowed to move your hips—indeed, you had to—and not fast, like in the cha-cha, but slow and wide. It gave me a sweet feeling to shift my weight first to one leg, then the other, hold still for a moment, then after the hesitation take a step to the right, away from my partner, controlled but full of tension. I loved the solo spin, the movement into free space, the geometry of the whole thing, and the possibility you both had to take a long look at each other before you came together as a couple again. This was the dance that made me feel powerful, irresistible, completely centered, and yet focused on him at every moment.

He was a quick learner. He watched the teacher attentively but stayed glued to my side. As we danced the first steps, his eyes were on my waist and my legs, and he let himself be led unresistingly by the pressure in my outstretched hand. When the music finally started—they had a real band playing, and the drummer teased out the long, slow beat with his brushes—from the very first moment it was magical. I almost forgot him, but when I did look at him, he seemed happy.

We always had a bit of an argument about who kissed whom first. Certainly it wasn't my first kiss—I was, after all, already eighteen and fundamentally not shy. But still I don't think I would have had the courage to initiate a first kiss with a man, even if there was darkness and a hedge of roses and everything was moving toward an embrace. Yet he said he would never have dared if I hadn't made the first move and only later, too late, did it occur to me that even back then he was beginning to push the responsibility for things onto me. All the same, it was wonderful. His breath was sweet. We stood there for a long time, just like that, almost without moving; we were almost the same height.

I made it a secret immediately. First, because I simply wasn't sure if I would ever hear from him again. So I just shrugged when Ulrike asked how the evening had gone, and I was monosyllabic with my mother. I tried not to think about him, and wasn't unsuccessful. I left the house at eight in the morning and a quarter of an hour later I was entering the big iron gateway surmounted with Ulrike's father's name in letters of wrought iron. I had long since given up any thought of further studies or acting school. Instead I had found my way to the sales department, where I was at the disposal of my boss, the heavy-breathing Dr. Brunner. Brunner had asthma, and he'd lost a hand in the war; he was thorough, and correct, and work was his whole life. When I arrived, he'd already been there long before me, and I rarely heard him telling his wife to come and pick him up at the end of the day; he often stayed late into the night. I accompanied him to meetings and took shorthand notes, and in the car he would answer my questions—I was allowed to sit beside him in the back—and seemed to be pleased that I was so keen. Steel didn't interest me particularly, but I liked working, and I had a real respect for the business where my father had worked for thirty years, after all. As for the question of what Dr. Hermann, wholesale and retail supplier of machine parts and tools, had actually done in the war, nobody thought about it back then. Now and again Brunner would ask me to wash his left hand; I got used to it. At home, I sometimes said I was my boss's right hand, because it amused me to watch my father's irritation, but soon nobody reacted anymore, and finally that's how Brunner himself talked about me. When I got to my desk in the morning, I wouldn't hear anything from him for quite some time; I'd deal with the in tray and the out tray, make coffee, and check through the internal mail for anything I could answer myself. After a year he started to say something sometimes, even if half jokingly, about some kind of career—by which he certainly meant a time frame of twenty or thirty years. That's the way things were then.

So in the morning I was alone quite a lot of the time. It suited me; the thing I'd hated most had been the first weeks in the typing pool, where I was nothing but an assistant: the whole day with seventeen other girls in an office, one more chicken in a flock of chickens, under constant observation. If I'd started daydreaming in there, the way I sometimes did in the days immediately following that evening, there would have been sideways looks full of complicity, clucks and sniggers, and whispered questions. Now there was no one to disturb me if I stared out of the window for minutes on end, or had to go looking for something I'd been holding only moments before. And even that soon stopped; it wasn't that I pushed him out of my head—he just sank into nothingness.

After ten days a letter arrived. No return address, just signed "Philip" and strangely brief. He proposed that we meet on Saturday evening, he would wait for me on the allée that led out of town, and hoped I'd be able to come. I no longer have the letter and cannot recall the exact wording, but I knew that I stared and stared at the meager sentences in which he'd managed to avoid using either the intimate or the formal form of "you." This made me happy, somehow.

I wore a light brown dress with a pattern in it of rose pink; the skirt was wide and had appliquéd pockets; I didn't even take a purse with me. I wore sandals on my feet, my arms and legs were bare: I went to him almost naked. Since the arrival of his letter, I was dreaming again, I imagined our kisses, I heard every bird that sang and every leaf that rustled, I hummed along to every hit song, I was in harmony with the whole world. I worked well and with real concentration, I had enough strength for ten—and yet as I turned into the allée my knees were knocking and my hands were thrust into the pockets of my skirt until they almost tore them. But he was already standing there.

He was already standing there, just as he would on almost every subsequent evening; he was leaning against a beech tree and waiting for me; he was always there first, and not once did we exchange a word of greeting.

At the beginning we didn't know what to say and later we kissed at once behind the great beech tree in the lonely allée. It led to a large village, which was now also accessible by a brand-new road, so we almost never saw another human being. We walked as far as the edge of the village and back again, then again, and sometimes we went further, through the woods to the old game-keeper's house, where there was a little bar. I no longer have any idea what we talked about, though we must have talked now and then in the whole long summer that followed. I must have told him about myself, my parents, the way they were at home, about the end of my dreams, my work and my boss, my friends, and how I met Ulrike. We talked about Ulrike a lot, because she'd brought us together, and because she was the only person we both knew.

At the same time, Ulrike and I weren't seeing each other anymore. I sometimes brooded over when we actually used to meet and why we no longer did so. Did she in some way intuit the relationship she'd set into motion? I didn't meet her again until everything was different, everything—or at least me.

I got his second letter right after our first rendezvous. On Monday morning it was in the mail, and I read it when I came home for lunch. There was a poem along with it that I've forgotten, but back then I learned it by heart and looked in the encyclopedia to learn everything I could about the man who wrote it; he was an Austrian named Lenau. It was easy for me to memorize the verses, but they seemed to me to be stale, gray, and paltry by comparison with my actual feelings and sensations as I walked under trees and held his hand. I had always thought that poetry was not worth much because it was hopelessly exaggerated; now my reservations were reversed: I thought, if that's all the poets have to say, it's totally inadequate, a tepid half-representation of reality. When I told him this—it must have been that same evening, because in those days I never could keep anything to myself—he was startled, and his disappointment showed; I think he was hurt that I didn't value his ideas. But when I explained to him, he finally looked relieved, and that was the last poem he ever copied out for me.

We were carried along by a kind of bliss. I never had a very good memory, but even back then I had no idea by Tuesday of what we had talked about on Monday night; I was no longer sure whether it had rained or not, or whether he had worn a white shirt, or how often we had walked up the road and back again. I saw the shimmering in the air, and sparks of light scintillating on the river, I still had the lingering smell in my nostrils of the trees we had leaned against, my lips could still taste the grass we had used to tickle each other, my body retained the memory of the hollow we sat in as we kissed, I could feel the cloth his shirt was made of, I could have put words to the texture of the air through which we walked—but I could no longer say whether I had really told him how old I was or what my father did at Hermann's or how my bedroom at home looked or what I liked most to eat. We didn't need things to keep us busy and I no longer had any idea how we spent our time; I remember our happiness, but I don't remember the shape it took.

My mother trusted me completely. She saw me go out in the evenings and come back happy, and that was enough for her. I don't know what she told my father, but he never asked me any questions, and so I didn't have to lie.

His letters began to change. At first they were all about him and me, then they became confessions. How lonely he was—beyond anything I could imagine. He didn't feel loved, he described his stepfather with absolute contempt. The man had a heart as cold as iron, all he could do was hand out orders and punishments. His brother meant nothing to him. His mother had gradually become a stranger—her weakness had made her incapable of defending him against his stepfather. The only thing she cared about was peace and quiet.

I was already head over heels, a hopeless case, before I learned his full name.

From a third party. It was Ilse, my friend from elementary school days, who passed us on her bike one day in a group of other kids. I bumped into her two weeks later at the baker's, and she made a remark that I didn't understand at first. That I'd made a really terrific catch, or some such thing. Philip was sufficiently good-looking to justify an observation like that, but there was an undertone in her voice that made me uneasy. Then she looked at me in shock. Was I saying that a Rhienäcker wasn't the biggest catch in all of our town of L.? I looked at her round, red face, and I didn't have a moment's doubt that she was telling the truth. I didn't ask her how she knew him, because I didn't want her to know how confused I was. I forgot the bread and went home.

We saw each other again that evening. He gave me the simplest of answers, namely that he thought I already knew. That he would never have realized that first evening that I hadn't taken in his name—at least that's what he said—and later on there wouldn't have been any reason to mention his last name again. And besides, it wasn't going to play any role in things: we loved each other. I didn't ask what was going to come of it now.

That was a question I only asked myself. I was the daughter of a minor employee who lived in a tract house he'd just finished paying off, my mother didn't even read the newspaper, on Saturdays my father went to the tavern and played Skat and my mother canned beans for the winter. The Rhienäckers owned a large estate outside town, Philip's real father was a pilot who'd been killed in the war, parties took place out at their house that were featured in the illustrated magazines. I could sing and dance, I was good at drawing, I was considered a beauty, and I could imagine all sorts of things. But how I would introduce my parents and the Rhienäcker family to one another was one thing I could not imagine at all.

We didn't discuss it. I didn't want to destroy anything and I put my faith in him. He was so sure in his affection, so focused on me in all his gentleness that I didn't want to think about anything except that this was how it would always be. In fall he would start his studies again, in two years he'd be finished, and we would get married. He spoke of his family with such scorn that I worried only for him, never for us.

He gave me a ring of thin woven bands of gold.

Then came his last letter. It was the day before we were due to have our last rendezvous before he left for M.

I must have fainted. When I regained consciousness, I was lying on the bed and a doctor was staring down at me, looking grim. When he asked me if I could speak, the question struck me as meaningless; I thought I was in the middle of a dream. Which was also why I wasn't at all surprised that I couldn't speak; all I wanted to do was wake up again. It was annoying not being able to speak, but at the same time I was so tired that what I wanted was to sleep, a long, long sleep, in spite of this strange dream in which my parents were sitting at my bedside with worried faces, my mother in floods of tears, my father in silent perplexity. The doctor finally turned away and went out with my parents, and I was relieved that now I could go back to sleep.

It was some time before I understood that I really couldn't speak. I remembered Philip's letter and the way I read it and then there was nothing more after that. My mother must have found it and read it, for she didn't ask any questions, and anyway, what was there left to ask? The doctors in the sanatorium wanted me to tell them what I remembered and what Philip had written, but I didn't tell them. They said it was important to talk about it if I was to get better, but I found it more important not ever to talk about it at all. And perhaps I was ashamed that I had believed him in the first place, for suddenly I was convinced that he had been betraying me from the very beginning, that he hadn't wanted to be bored all summer, that perhaps he had even had a bet with his friend that he would seduce me. Today I see it differently; I think he was both weak and soft as a human being, and that he just didn't want to think about things any more than I did. And that when he told them at home that he wanted to marry me, it all of a sudden became blindingly clear that the whole idea was absurd. I don't think for a minute that money was the deciding factor. But back then I thought otherwise. Back then, in the sanatorium, I did my exercises and wrote little letters to my parents. In the evenings I read; the library was quite extensive, and I chewed my way through it all: slowly, easily pleased, sometimes with real involvement. I was content to watch unroll in front of me unhappy love stories and the other ones, novels from France and America and Germany and one that began in a country house in England and ended in South America. I made no distinctions as to good or bad, not even as to whether the stories were exciting or not; there was something undemanding in this reading, it was like the grazing of an animal. Much later I realized that I really must have been ill, because otherwise nobody would have sent a girl like me, on company insurance and at a time of full employment, to a sanatorium for a couple of months, to be supervised as she ate and spoke and read and did exercises in the open air. But I didn't think about that at the time. I didn't think much at all. I saw that the sky was blue and I saw that the place was beautiful when someone pointed this out to me. I saw that my clothes were too big for me. I saw that they served good cheese at suppertime. I knew that my parents loved me. I saw, when I looked in the mirror, that I was still beautiful—a bit thinner, a bit translucent somehow, a little too "transfigured" for a girl from the provinces, but beautiful all the same. The doctors had asked my parents to give me something to bring along that mattered to me. And what my mother chose was the mirror, my only small inheritance from my grandmother, who had died young; it was a valuable ornament, oval, with a beautifully gilded frame, that always hung in my room and that I often used. The mirror was not much larger than my head, and when I stood in front of it to comb my hair—a rebellious tangle of curls—I could see the hollow in the center of my collarbone. The doctors thought her choice was a wonderful idea; the sanatorium made it an exercise, one just for me, to look at myself in this mirror for ten minutes every day. I was supposed to see myself as a pretty young girl with a whole life in front of me. But what I saw and knew eased nothing inside me. The blue sky gave me no joy, my bagging clothes didn't alarm me, the cheese tasted of nothing in my mouth. That my parents loved me was just a given. Sad for them, I thought, but that's all it was—a thought; I didn't feel its truth, any more than I could feel anything for myself.

That's the way it was for a long time. I went back home, I started working again. In the meantime Herr Brunner had taken on a new right hand and I moved into the distribution division. On instructions from my parents, I started going to a bowling club. Once I met Ulrike on the street and both of us stopped and neither of us knew what to say. I sewed new dresses with my mother. On Saturday evenings I sat between Hans and Freddy and Ernst on a long bench, opposite me sat Margit and Ursula, and Ernst told one of his stories, and when the others laughed, I laughed too. I went with Ernst to Irmi's, and she was the first person in those days, perhaps the only one, I cared about at all.

Then one Saturday I read in the paper that Philip was engaged to someone named Liane Westerhoff, whom I didn't know but whose name I did know since there was a banking firm in F. called Westerhoff. The wedding was to take place on the Rhienäcker estate.

The other thing was in the paper today. The pedestrian had suffered fatal injuries, there was a bulletin out about a hit-and-run driver; if anyone had seen anything, please to call the police.

But no one could have seen anything. It was raining, it was almost dark—not the weather you'd choose for going for a walk. Certainly not along an arterial road with no shops and no trees for the dogs. No one could have seen anything.

■ ■ ■

At the time, a lot of people knew about us. I told absolutely no one, but all the same the news made the rounds. Maybe my mother lost her nerve and shared a confidence with somebody—and the somebody could have been the baker's wife, a neighbor, or even Ulrike, who came to visit us even this year at Christmas. Probably Ilse hadn't been able to keep her mouth shut—and indeed why should she, it was not a secret she had any obligation to hide. A nervous breakdown didn't belong in our circle. Such a thing required a cause, and the cause certainly existed. When I came back, I noticed a general awkwardness; I hadn't worked out anything that I could produce by way of an explanation. So I said nothing at all about what had gone on, and that was itself a kind of confession. The only thing that everyone believed was that I really wasn't pregnant. My mother in her desperation must have showed people my letters from the sanatorium. A pregnant daughter was bad, but not what you'd call a calamity; a pregnant daughter who came home without a baby was a scandal for the rest of her life.

This announcement in the paper woke me up. My first emotion was fury, my second was rage. The fury was cold and involuntary, the rage was hot, a living thing. "You shouldn't be the first!" I said to myself, as if this would make any difference. I worked out how long it would be until the wedding, I reckoned six months, maybe less. Certainly while it was still summer, a year after our summer, while the grass was still fragrant and you could dance the night away in the great inner courtyard of the estate while it was still time for crickets to be singing and champagne under the open sky. Perhaps Liane Westerhoff was not very attractive and perhaps she couldn't dance, but she too must have her dreams and make a wish that as she came out of the chapel in her white dress she would have the blessing not just of the church but of the heavens as well.

▦ ▦ ▦

I also wonder why he was on foot; perhaps he had had to leave his car because of some engine problem. He certainly drove ostentatious cars, but he couldn't afford really good ones—so they would most likely be machines with sporty bodywork and tuned-up engines and flashy extras; cars like that are temperamental and sometimes just won't go. It was probably secondhand when he bought it; a car from F., previously involved in an accident, resprayed once, new radio and additional headlights, leather seats included in price. Impressive for quick tours on the weekend, but not very heavy-duty, and in our damp countryside things rust quickly, or the ignition gives up. This is no place for sports cars.

■ ■ ■

I didn't have a plan right away. It was more that in the very second after I read the announcement everything became inevitable; a decision had been made as if independently of me; there was no more room for questions, now the only thing left was action. As I went with Ernst to Irmi's that evening, I still felt utterly empty, and yet determined all the way, and when he took me home from there, I chattered to him as if that's what we'd always done. It wasn't until sometime in the night that I imagined our life together.

My parents would go back to S. to my mother's sisters and my grandfather, who lived alone in his little apartment—this had been clear for years already. My father, who had had a modest career at Hermann's Wholesale and Retail, had never felt at home in the area, and my mother had spent all those years just waiting for the moment when she could sell the little house and move back to where her family lived. My father's pension would start in two years—too long for me to wait and then go with them, and besides, I didn't want to go back to S. at their side as an old maid, to my married cousins with their conversations about their children and holidays in the Tyrol and their long-established jealousy of me—beautiful, popular Margarethe, who could draw and sing and dance and wanted to go to drama school and who still hadn't done any more than be an office girl abandoned by her boyfriend, with a nervous breakdown. I would marry Ernst and live with him and Irmi; in spite of everything, Ernst looked good, he treated me with real consideration, he earned a good living, he was a dear good man who wouldn't deny me anything, and Irmi was simply a treasure. I imagined how nice it would be to have her around, and I imagined Ernst's dazzled gratitude that he wouldn't have to leave his mother, the war widow, alone, but would be allowed to bring her with him into the marriage. I would go on working, in the evenings we would often be with friends—nothing would become of my dancing now—and when we came home, Irmi would be there, a source of life and good cheer. Perhaps we would have a child. Above all, we would have a big wedding, this summer already, in a banqueting hall with a chapel and lots of guests; I would send out printed invitations and place a notice in the paper: "Congratulatory visits after 1 p.m.; Haus Blumenthal." I would design my dress myself and buy the silk for it, even if it meant driving to F. to find the perfect material. I was going to be the first.

From that moment on, it was a form of ice-cold delirium. When I awoke next morning, I allowed myself an instant's reflection—but my mind was made up. I had enormous willpower, and I had no desire to stop myself. I was grateful for the rage that swallowed everything up: the exhaustion of the last six months, the sense of indifference and alienation and the feeling of not being at home in the world. I thought of all that and was terrified, I did not want on any account to be the Margarethe who lived through those days ever again. And it really wasn't important whether it was Ernst or someone else; I could steer Ernst, it wasn't hard to tell this much, he had his quirks but no real character flaws, and his disability made him so grateful. Philip didn't know him, which was neither important nor particularly an advantage; he would read the notice in the newspaper and it would hit home, the way the announcement of his engagement had hit home with me, maybe even more so: I would be going first, he wouldn't be able to think I'd be standing on our riverbank on his wedding day looking over at the brick walls of the Rhienäcker estate with tears in my eyes. I'd be well embarked on my honeymoon, to Paris, why not?

I met Ernst that same evening at the bowling club; he walked me home and it came about quite naturally that we talked about the future. At first he couldn't believe that this was about him, and I had to make very clear that the way was open for him. He was so beside himself with happiness that I was rather ashamed—but then I told myself defiantly that nevertheless someone was being made happy and it was my doing, and there couldn't be anything so bad about making someone that happy. Irmi would be thrilled too, she'd liked me at once; according to Ernst on several occasions, she was almost as much in love with me as he was, but there was something about this that humbled me: she wasn't just proud of me, she really loved me. For Ernst I was a trophy, some equivalent of a cup you win at bowling, the most beautiful girl in his circle, who never let anyone near her, who never cooed and flirted—Margarethe, who, everyone said, had something special about her. That she wanted to marry him struck him as so unbelievable that he didn't try to figure out any cause for it—it had something of the quality of a miracle, and it would have been blasphemy to search for causes or weigh the merits that had made him worthy of her. He took it as a gift without measure, a lottery he had won without a ticket—and perhaps I should have been moved by this at the time, for his gratitude bore no trace of faintheartedness, no doubt, no mistrust, nothing that forced me into the embarrassment of an explanation. This gratitude was pure and unalloyed, larger than himself in the way a child's gratitude can be, but it didn't move me, I accepted it without thought; it wasn't the point. But it strengthened my resolve and made what followed easier. Now there was nothing more to it; even my parents, although astonished, were relieved and happy. She's leading with her heart, my mother must have thought. But I was leaving it behind instead.

■ ■ ■

I could have decided otherwise. There was a second's reflection, a tiny fraction of my existence, in which I could have changed things. All I had to do was stay still, do nothing, and the moment would have passed. He would have crossed the street; he hadn't even noticed me, he was waiting quite calmly for the light to change—which was surprising in and of itself, because it was raining and almost dark, and most people would have turned and looked and then crossed. But he stood there waiting calmly, perhaps plunged in thought, and then he set off quite unworriedly. And why should he have been worried? He hadn't spotted me, hadn't recognized me, and even if he had, the most he would have done was wave hello, but I'm not even sure he'd have done that.

■ ■ ■

Now everything began to unroll smoothly. We quickly found a little house with a garden, Irmi contributed her small savings, and because both of us were earning, we could manage the investment over the long haul. It was at the other end of town, so I drove to work at Hermann's; Ernst walked to the branch office of the savings bank where he'd been employed ever since he was a trainee. The three of us had breakfast together every morning and we ate together at night; then Ernst and I sometimes went out again, or we played Skat or watched TV. We often had company; Irmi liked to cook and made people welcome, in winter there were stews or pot roasts, in summer we sat out in the garden and cooked on the grill while the radio played; we listened to national league games, I made marmalade with Irmi and over the years I laid out a kitchen garden. I was never a good housewife, nor did that sort of thing interest me particularly; Irmi took all that over for me, she absolutely loved cleaning, tried out new recipes, and did the ironing. I warmed myself on her; it was like sitting in a car when it's cold out and the windshield slowly fogs over from your warm breath. Except that I wasn't doing the breathing, it was Irmi beside me and maybe also Ernst in the backseat. He was brimming over with happiness and it made him less silly; perhaps he needed less applause now that he'd married me, and we got on well with each other. My parents visited us three or four times a year; they never asked me how I was, and if they had, I wouldn't have known what to say. In a department store advertisement I'd have looked good, like a woman testing a new vacuum cleaner or trying on a new hat and liking what she sees in the mirror. I did miss reading a bit, but there was simply no time for it, not until I became pregnant.

From the very beginning I had to stay lying flat; I had bleeding from time to time and the doctor said sternly that I should spare myself all possible activity and rest as much as I could—a first pregnancy at twenty-eight wasn't unproblematic in any case. So I stayed at home and lay in bed or on the sofa while Irmi ran the house around me. I often felt ill, and the only thing that seemed to help was eating, so I munched on nuts or pretzels or chocolate, drank lemonade along with them, and was soon as heavy as if I were about to give birth. Ernst was even more loving during this period; he came home with candy or flowers for me and entertained me with stories from the savings bank. I'm the money doctor, he said sometimes, I know more about people than an internist, I know what they want and what they won't be able to manage for themselves, I know how they plan their lives, even their deaths, because we administer estate things as well, like the savings accounts that the grandchildren or the daughters get to evade the sons-in-law. Of course Ernst was only dealing with little people; people with real money didn't start by using a savings bank, and if they did, then certainly not in L., where a small row house with a garden like the one we were paying off was the maximum one could aspire to. Ernst wanted a girl, which surprised me a little; I thought all men wanted a son. I'm lucky with women, he said, looking happily at both me and Irmi, and his wish was granted.

Daniela sometimes repelled me a little. As a little girl, she would look around her if she fell, and if she saw someone watching me she would begin to cry noisily. She was always on the lookout for us, not because she wanted to be with us but because she seemed to be calculating what attitude to take. At the swimming pool a mother came to me, holding her little daughter by the hand; the girl was perhaps two years old and had bite marks on her arm. That was your daughter, said the woman, more shocked than angry. I called Daniela and questioned her, but she just shook her little strawberry blond head and wouldn't look at anyone. What upset me most was that I believed the woman; I could recognize that Daniela, at age four, was capable of it. There was something sly about her, and I kept racking my brains about where she got it from: certainly not from my parents or Irmi or Ernst, which left only Heinz-Günther. I didn't want to hurt Irmi; I wanted to see if she would bring it up herself. Perhaps other children were like that too, perhaps I was too critical.

Ernst, of course, spoiled the child; he was as much in love with Daniela as he had been with me when we were first married. Maybe I didn't spend enough time taking care of her; when it came down to it, I was relieved that I could soon start work again and Daniela would stay with Irmi, where she was in the best hands. Irmi never uttered a word of criticism, but sometimes I thought I could read concern in her eyes. We bought a dog, because we thought maybe Daniela lacked company. It was a spaniel, a gentle creature that allowed himself patiently to be ordered around by Daniela. From time to time she would lift him onto her lap and squeeze him so tightly that he struggled; when he tried to free himself, she seized him, took hold of his little muzzle and twisted his head toward her face: you're my dog, she said, you do as I say! I felt sorry for the animal, and pinned my hopes on school—perhaps she would lose some of her roughness there along with a level of self-esteem that I felt was exaggerated.

But Daniela was not sociable, nor did she become so. What she liked best was being at home, where she played the princess: all our guests would bring things for her, she switched from one lap to the next and flirted with Ernst's friends. Above all she was bewitched by pretty clothes; she would take a long time in the mornings deciding what to wear, and there were exhausting discussions if she didn't like a pullover or if she had to wear trousers because it was raining. I tried to admonish myself to be more patient with her and to go along with her, but deep down she disturbed me, and I don't think we liked each other. Sometimes she sat in front of my three-sided mirror in the bedroom and painted her face with total concentration, turning this way and that and looking at herself from every angle. She was slender and charming, liked to go to the ballet and show us her newest pirouettes in the living room in the evening; that was when she was in her element. I bought a piano and we both played it, but her ambition quickly evaporated, and for a long time it was impossible to interest her in anything at all. She didn't like me to touch her.

■ ■ ■

A pity that I didn't see his face. I would have liked to know if he recognized me, if at the last moment he realized what was happening to him. But it was dark and it all happened very quickly. I felt a dull impact, I saw him go flying through the air—but perhaps I only imagined that, there was almost nothing to be seen except the headlights and in them the glistening pewter-colored ribbons of rain. Nor did I hear a thing. Perhaps I was too agitated.

■ ■ ■

They say the years pass quicker as one grows older, but even back then I felt that everything was standing still. Daniela got bigger, Ernst got fatter. Irmi hardly aged at all, but she had to take blood pressure pills, which she kept forgetting. I don't remember any particular events, I see us as if we're all in photos: fifteen years in the same three-piece suite in the living room while its covers gradually got darker and darker until we had to buy a new set. The wooden bowl from Spain that held the pretzels; a small tin jug that the toothpicks stood in; the cork mats. Ernst trained himself to stop smoking. In the place where he always sat, the carpet in front of the sofa was worn right through. The window onto the garden was always open, and over time the room became darker, because the fir tree began to cut the light. Irmi sat in her armchair with a reading lamp next to it, doing her handwork while she watched TV. She knitted dresses for Daniela, crocheted shawls and coverlets, and for Ernst she made pullovers and jackets that fit his new proportions. He was still a really good-looking man; as the years went on he talked louder, because he had grown used to the fact that his clients paid attention to him.

In the meantime I had become for all intents and purposes the head of the sales department. My boss was a sickly man and the company didn't want to demote him, but it was clear to everyone that I was doing the actual work, and I was well paid too. I still liked going to the office, even if the business had changed almost completely from the one I'd known as a child. Old Dr. Hermann had died, and nobody now handed out the Christmas money to the employees in person; the firm had been bought by someone else and the really important business was conducted from F. I couldn't speak any foreign languages, I hadn't used my English since high school, and it was clear to me that I wouldn't be able to advance myself much further. I drove a fast car—I'd always loved that—and now and then Ernst and I would meet Hans and the others for a weekend by the Rhine or the Moselle; we'd have a wine-tasting and drink too much and then we'd drive home again. Once Freddy tried to kiss me when Ernst had already gone into the hotel and we were the last to stagger back; I let myself go along to begin with, but then I started to laugh. Not only because I was drunk but because I also found the hopelessness of the whole thing funny. Were we supposed to tiptoe out through the hall in the middle of the night, with Sabine asleep in his bed and Ernst in mine, and then grope each other on some bench by the Moselle?

■ ■ ■

It must have been the third of May when we met, the day before Daniela's birthday. There was to be a party in the garden for her friends, and in the evening we wanted to go to the movies. The day before was a Saturday and our choir was giving a concert at the pump house; a major program, from Handel to Lehár, as part of the one-thousand-year anniversary of the town, speeches before and dancing to follow. The tickets were expensive, there was a large buffet, and I had bought a new evening dress, dark blue, almost floor-length, with a border of shimmering silver chiffon. I had lost ten pounds to look right in it. We were sitting fairly close to the front at a table with Becker the choirmaster, and we were on our second bottle of champagne, when he came over to us.

I had noticed him already. He was very tall and held himself erect; his dinner jacket was just a little too tight, but he moved elegantly and I liked the way he held his cigarette. He didn't draw on it hungrily, nor did he neglect it; he seemed rather to concentrate on it while talking to the woman opposite. They were sitting at the next table, right by the dance floor, but the band wasn't playing yet. He came up to Becker, pulled over a chair, and apparently said something nice to him; I saw Becker gesturing and looking incredibly pleased, and then he was pointing at me. I raised my eyes to his as he smiled down at me.

Daniela would be thirteen next day, I had turned forty, I knew I still looked good, and I was Becker's best soprano. Next to me was my husband, opposite were Freddy and Sabine, and it was promising to become a lively evening. As he introduced himself to us, he seemed polite and charming, a little touch of the salesman, maybe a real estate agent. He praised our program and said enough to suggest that he wasn't completely ignorant about the music; he asked about particular details of how the voices were being led and said finally that he had once sung too. He was, he said, the new head of our local department of culture, and hence particularly interested in activities like ours; it sounded less rehearsed than it does to me now, for he was lively and witty, and struck up an immediate rapport with Sabine. Eventually he went back to his table, and when the band began to play I saw him dancing quite energetic waltzes with a young blonde. I shared Freddy with Sabine, because of course Ernst didn't dance, but most of the time I stayed sitting beside him and watched the dance floor.

I didn't see him coming because he approached us by way of the corridor, and he asked Ernst with a wink if he might be allowed to abduct me. They were playing a foxtrot, and you had to talk, because the floor was so full that you couldn't move. He immediately had lots to say, mentioned his secretary—the young blonde—and his wife, who, alas, had fallen ill, but he couldn't cancel an event like this because it was his job. I didn't know whether he was joking or not, I had no idea what the obligations of the head of a department of culture were; I was only aware that he was having a good time, and so was I. Something attracted me to him at once, although it also made me uneasy; it was his dexterity, his physical suppleness, everything around him felt suddenly light and easy, I suddenly felt lighter too, as though I'd lost far more than ten pounds. I like your perfume, he said in my ear, and I blushed because I hadn't put any on, which, when I thought about it, made his remark even more flattering—and when I thought about it a second time, I wondered if he knew that, because he was grinning at me so conspiratorially, so I told him what I was thinking.

I always told him the truth. I didn't often take the trouble to lie to Ernst, but I also didn't make any confessions to him either, because everything I said would have had to begin with a lie. Things between us were the way they were, no amount of talking would change anything, and complications didn't interest him. His life's goal was to be comfortable, he was as transparent in that regard as a glass of water, and he only thought about people in any serious way if they troubled his comfort. He was satisfied once he had found a way to fit his thoughts to events—that Freddy had troubles in his business and that was why he was sometimes so grumpy, or that Monica didn't visit us anymore because she had a drinking problem. That was all he needed, and after that he could wait like a Buddha until circumstances readjusted themselves into the pattern that was most comfortable for him. He sometimes picked up my novels from the bedside table and read the flap copy to himself under his breath and then asked me in genuine astonishment why I would be so interested in the collapse of some noblewoman's marriage in the last century—who then went and died of heartbreak, what's more. Irmi knew me well, but she asked me nothing; it wasn't her way and I was grateful to her for that. I had a few friends who shared confidences with me—little flirtations, secret worries, or simply how you tried to get your husband to buy the Persian lamb coat that he'd flatly refused you. I had nothing similar to tell; I could buy the fur coat myself, but Ernst would have given it to me without hesitation because what he wanted above all was domestic peace, and a Persian lamb coat would not have struck him as too high a price to pay. He had got what he wanted—me—and that made him tractable and even more patient than he was anyway; there was nothing he wished for anymore, but this didn't kill him, it was something he lived with, the way a dog lives with a slowly enlarging liver until one day in the middle of a beautiful dream he dies.

■ ▓ ▓

It was from the newspaper that I first learned that he really was dead. "Died on the spot" is what it said in both the first and the second article, in exactly the same words, as if they'd simply written the announcement out twice. He must have broken his neck. I think internal bleeding does not cause death instantaneously. The number of investigations into hit-and-run accidents had been rising steadily in recent years, according to the newspaper. But what could they do, when there were no witnesses? They couldn't examine every car within a thirty-five-mile radius. And that wouldn't get them anywhere either.

▦ ▦ ▦

We danced with each other twice again that evening; as we left at one-thirty in the morning, he was still on the dance floor; I don't think he noticed our departure. We were all slightly tipsy, and Sabine took me aside on the stairs because she was a little smitten by him. A ladies' man, she said, he'd go far! If Freddy didn't watch her the way he did, it would be worth committing a sin. But that's how Sabine always talked, in part because she wanted to annoy Freddy, and also naturally because she was bored in L. I got four children out of sheer boredom! she said sometimes; at the same time she was a model mother and as solid as Ernst, only she didn't want to admit it. I didn't say anything back to her; I thought: a night's sleep and that would be that, in the end that's how it always was; you're over forty, I told myself, your daughter will be thirteen tomorrow—no, today—and you haven't been up to flirting for years now, if you ever could.

Weeks passed. Of course I couldn't flirt, I'd never learned how; I had never learned to take anything lightly at all, to just try something, to take a risk. All I could do was endure, I could do that well, endure everything: Ernst and his habits, Rudi Carrell who couldn't pronounce his *r*'s, Daniela's attacks of bad temper, and Irmi, who wasn't going to live forever. I could endure anything. Weeks went by, and of course I didn't see him again, and in the mornings in the car I thought to myself that it was for the best, for I wasn't cut out for an affair, and he was a man who went in for them, which was something I'd understood right away. In the evenings as I drove home, I said it to myself all over again; I ate supper with Irmi and Ernst and Daniela, then we sat and watched TV together while Daniela listened to music through earphones in her room or talked on the phone with her friends or just lay there and stared at the posters she'd pinned up on the walls. I would have liked to do that too, but I was also relieved that I wasn't allowed to—it was something you were allowed if you were a teenager, dreaming your way into another world with total abandon.

■ ■ ■

The thing keeps getting more play. Yet another article today, with another appeal for help with the police inquiries. They were taking his death very seriously. They didn't know it was a blessing he no longer existed.

■ ■ ■

There was a summer ball as well. We were doing a performance again, this time in Haus Blumenthal. This time the only place for the better sort of people was actually open to anyone who could pay the entry fee, and here came the polyester coats, the skirts and shirtwaists, the little cars, the men in dark suits who'd never owned a dinner jacket—in short, here came us and our friends.

But the head of the department of culture came too: he gave a little speech, made a few easy jokes that everyone could understand, and quoted from a poem by Lenau. He came to our table, he sat with us for an hour and his wife, once again, wasn't with him, but neither was his secretary. He asked me to dance a couple of times, and said he was so glad to see me again, but he certainly didn't notice anything about me. He pushed a piece of paper at me that I didn't read, and later when I was alone in the toilet it said tomorrow evening, six o'clock, Ferdinand House—it was an excursion place by the river—and I stared into the mirror in helpless shock and tore the little note into even littler pieces and I didn't know what I would do.

But of course I went; it wasn't hard, it was right after work, I had called home and said something about overtime, and when I was already on the road I became aware that my knees were trembling and knocking, and my foot was twitching up and down; I juddered my way down the long allée like a learner-driver trying to manage a ninety-horsepower engine, and that wasn't far from the truth.

He stayed in his car when he saw me drive up; it wasn't until I had parked and got out that he finally came over to me and we walked immediately into the woods as if that had been prearranged, and he took my arm at once and as we walked around the first bend he stopped and said Margarethe and stroked my modestly arranged hair and I felt my shoes sinking into the earth and my life along with them. He hadn't been prepared for this to happen to him again, was the first thing he said, and I said the same. I didn't want any explanations right now, I wanted a total mental blank. Despite this or perhaps because of it, I talked about Philip; they were the same woods, after all, and it was my past life. I told the whole story of Philip and me; it was only when he wanted to know how I saw the whole thing now that I realized that I had been thinking about it for more than twenty years without knowing. I had measured every marriage in our circle—except for my own—against what ours should have been, I had looked at every man as a deviation from Philip, he had been my original man, the way there was supposed to be the original meter measured out somewhere in Paris; I had measured every affair I'd heard about against my own experience, my own love, and our love for each other, and I had measured every spring against our spring, and every summer too. This was why nothing had been able to pose a real threat to me. I wavered in my judgment of Philip; I didn't want to reach the end. And now the end was going to be Michael, forty-three, dark-haired, head of the department of culture in L., married, two children. He was to be the end in order for something new to begin.

Of course the only possibility was to use hotels, and of course we couldn't stay in the town. Sometimes we had to drive great distances to find a place; too out of the way for other people from L., too expensive or too cheap, too unknown or only for traveling salesmen.

The first time we made a rendezvous was three weeks after that walk; in the meantime there had been only phone calls, during which my voice often failed or I had to hang up quickly because someone was coming in. I could never call back, because his secretary came on the line first; I had to wait for him the way an animal waits for food. I didn't feel humiliated, I felt hollowed out, as if I were made of paper or thin cloth. I was too nervous to eat, I pushed food around my plate in the evenings and murmured that I didn't feel well; I didn't drink anymore either, for fear I might dream of him out loud; I only smoked a lot more than usual, because in some strange way it kept me together. I paid great attention at work, but still documents kept disappearing only to turn up in unexpected places, and I was continually mislaying things, keys and sunglasses and my driver's license, cigarettes, lighter, dry cleaner's slips and shopping lists, even my shoes. I went to the doctor and got myself a prescription for an upset stomach—that was how I explained away my restlessness and my loss of weight and the fact that I was more nervous than usual. Only Daniela looked at me from time to time as though she suspected something.

▣ ▣ ▣

I drove the car to a car wash right away. The one just before the entrance to the highway; I wash the car there at least twice a month, vacuum off the mats and the seats and buy magazines, cigarettes, and something to nibble; sometimes I also get the oil changed or the tire pressure checked. I like taking care of those things, the people who work there know me and we often chat to each other. I bought a *Brigitte* that evening—which means it was a Wednesday—and a *Madame,* licorice candy and a cloth to clean the windshield, and at the checkout counter I also talked with the woman who ran the place about the continuing bad weather. I wasn't in the least agitated; perhaps it was the shock, perhaps it was a sort of pride at having really done something, and done it right; my voice certainly hadn't changed and I behaved quite normally. Then I drove my usual way home; Ernst, of course, was already there, watching a political program, Irmi was beside him in the armchair, knitting; neither of them was surprised; I wasn't coming back any later than I did when I had something to take care of.

■ ■ ■

When I got to the hotel the first time, I could hardly breathe. It was a mild later summer day, with no wind; I had had my hair cut, and was glad it wasn't raining; I was wearing doe-brown suede pumps and a wine-red two-piece that I'd bought a few days before. I had thought and thought about what underwear to wear—I was a little too old for black, at least that's how it seemed to me, and also I was afraid of seeming too common. Eventually I decided on a flesh-toned set; the bra unhooked in front, and my stockings were dark red. He hadn't arrived yet; I sat down on the terrace, ordered a glass of wine, and tried to wait. It was an excursion hotel in a valley off the beaten track; a stream ran by within hearing distance, and you could see the fortress to which they offered outings. The wine was too warm and there were lots of midges. Two tables away there was a loud group bent on having a good time and getting drunk: perhaps a bowling club. I could have been one of them, with Ernst and Freddy and Sabine and all the others, instead of which I was sitting here waiting for the man who was to become my lover, smoking to drive away the insects and looking at the time every three minutes. I had spun Ernst a story about visiting a branch office; it could get late, we'd be going on to dinner afterward in H. But I had to be home around midnight at the latest, and it was already almost eight o'clock. After half an hour, I thought of simply driving home, but I didn't want to be rescued by fate; I wanted something else from this man besides frantic phone calls and secret walks in the woods, I wanted to be in a room with him, I wanted to whisper because I wanted to, not because I had to.

That I would eventually cry out was something I hadn't imagined. I didn't care who heard, because I knew that we would never come back here, he'd said that already: never the same place twice. To begin with it was like a pinprick, without my being able to say why, it wasn't until I was driving back that I grasped that it was the plannedness that was disconcerting, a plan for us was good, but maybe the plan for us was part of some bigger plan, and I didn't want to be part of any plan whose goal wasn't me. When he reached for the cigarettes in his jacket, I pulled the sheet over my stomach and looked at the green-and-red-striped armchair in front of the bed on which my purse lay, and thought it was a relief that I didn't have to pay attention to the chair, I'd never see it again, it was a random piece of furniture, a little worn, a little gone in the seat, not as welcoming as Irmi's but also with a reading lamp behind it that stood with its big yellowish shade a little crooked. There was a glass ashtray advertising cigars, flat and triangular, like the ones you see in a bar. He set it on his stomach and lit up for both of us, and we lay there in silence, and I wondered how my hair looked. I raised my head to look in the mirror that was set into the cupboard door, and there was a middle-aged woman with dark hair and a flushed face, undone and serious at the same time; my image looked indistinct to me, but the mirror could have been old. It would have been the time for a declaration of love, but I didn't trust myself. His stomach looked flatter lying down; maybe mine did too. I realized I was waiting to see what his first words would be; it was like a test that he didn't know was happening. Only when he eventually felt around on the bedside table and said ten o'clock did I know that he would have passed any test; it didn't matter what he said, all I wanted was to see him again. I saw my underwear lying on the floor; he had undressed me slowly and stroked my skin with his fingertips; I had shivered and tried to look at him but I couldn't properly; I was too busy trying not to do anything wrong that first night, which was no proper night at all.

Later on it got better. I enjoyed crying out, I took physical pleasure in drawing him out, I would vanish into the bathroom and come back naked, or I would undress slowly in front of him; once I stood on a balcony with a range of foothills behind me in the dark and took all my clothes off; he stood inside the room and watched me, and then I sat on the stone balustrade and told him to come to me. Later we dragged the bedding onto the balcony and lay there smoking and drinking a bottle of champagne as we looked up at the sky and tried to find the Milky Way. I had brought a candle with me and it flickered wildly beside us, and though the floor of the balcony was very hard, we lay there for a long time. Another time, in F., we met at a hotel in the middle of town; the room was on the seventeenth floor, and from the bed we looked at the skyscrapers, lights were still going on and off at ten-thirty at night as we lay on top of each other and spoke with our lips touching; when I was half dressed, he undressed me again; he began with my stockings, without saying a word, and I felt myself slowly slide down onto the floor.

I could no longer distinguish between the smell of his body and my own, so I showered when I got home in the evening; so that it wouldn't be obvious, I did it every day and said I was having hot flashes. I found it quite funny,

myself, that I was making out I was suffering the menopause when I was actually feeling twenty, but the others
didn't seem to think anything of it. After these hours
with him I would put on a pair of pajamas and take
some novel to bed; I didn't read them, but I could turn
my back on Ernst and wait till I heard the noises he made
when he was asleep. He rolled onto his side, almost to
the edge, and let an arm hang out over the bed frame, his
breath rattled a little but soon steadied into a regular
rhythm; he would stay there, sound asleep and unmov-
ing, until the alarm went off, while I often twisted and
turned and thought about the time that had just been
and the next time and was glad that my side of the bed
faced the window, where I couldn't see much sky but at
least I could hear the hedge rustling in the wind and the
nut tree, right next to the wall, which had Daniela's
swing hanging from it.

■ ■ ■

An interview in the paper with the commissioner in
charge of the investigation. I wondered if they were making so much of the thing because there was nothing else
to report: a school sports day, the dedication of the new
offices in the chamber of commerce, here and there a
minor break-in and an alert about con men who were
apparently calling on people about their radio taxes so
that they could look around people's apartments that
they thought would be worth robbing when they got the

chance. It was unusual, said the newspaper, for information to be given out not by someone in the press department but by the official in charge himself. When I looked at his face, I knew why: the man was ambitious, he was not yet forty, he came from F., and he'd like to get out someday, so an unsolved hit-and-run wouldn't look good in his file.

■ ■ ■

I didn't make the same mistake again. I wanted to know everything about him, starting with his family. He didn't speak badly of his wife, which I immediately scored in his favor. He had told me her name already on that first walk, and it made our conversation easier; at least it was less unpleasant for me to talk about Karin instead of "your wife," and he also mentioned the names of his fourteen- and eight-year-old sons. He even showed me a photo, as if to interpose the three of them between us, the way Catholics make the sign of the cross when they encounter the devil, or a witch, come to that. I didn't know whether I should look at the picture, but he put it in my hand, and I examined it closely. Two children with flax-blond hair, chin-length, in bright-colored cross-striped sweaters; they looked harmless and their expressions were a little troubled; the background was a blue satin curtain. The mother, i.e., his wife, stood behind the two of them with a hand on each shoulder; she too was flax-blond, with a wide, slightly angular face, and radiated calm and energy as she looked straight into the camera. When was it taken, I asked, in order to have something to say, and he said it was about two years ago. At night I wondered if he had answered vaguely in order to spare my feelings or whether he really didn't know anymore, for a photo like that is usually a gift to mark a particular date: a birthday, Christmas, or the end of the school year. Karin's face hadn't stamped itself on my mind, she looked like a good mother, an attentive house-wife, or what in the business world would be called a Good Head; not easy to intimidate but easy to please. She must have been a really pretty girl when she was young, with her thick hair and her snub nose, her clear blue eyes and that rosy glow so common in her kind of healthy blond woman; now she looked a bit solid, not fat exactly but not graceful either; someone who couldn't be fazed by anything, but someone you'd rather pass on the escalator than stand behind that broad back waiting to see if she'd take a step of her own accord.

He even told me how they met; it was on a skiing trip in Austria, and they were in the same hotel; her par-ents were there too, and he was taking a vacation with a colleague from F., where he was still employed in the local government offices. In the evenings she sat alone in the bar; they had a drink together and discovered that they both knew some of the same people in F., where she had done her technical training. Her parents were quite reserved but were very solid people. The way he spoke of his father-in-law was almost worshipful; he was apparently a man who'd really proved himself as an entrepreneur after the war, but very approachable, good cardplayer, good drinker. He started with a little bakery, built it into a chain with more than fourteen shops, but he worked right up to his heart attack in the same first shop, because he was attached to it and that's where he was happiest. Karin had then taken over the business and managed it superbly—I had no idea what to say to all this; it would feel really stupid to praise Karin's dedication, but I also didn't want to put her down, and I couldn't shake the feeling that it wasn't the real story. That then emerged almost by the by; they'd got married when she was already pregnant, but he recounted this as if it were irrelevant, as if they'd have got married anyway and Thomas only speeded things up. I recognized this from my friends, at a certain point you really came to believe this, and it was the same feeling I'd had when I took Ernst—it had to be someone, and in the long run was there really all that much difference? We all wanted a little house and a garden and children and trips to Spain and to grow old in peace, and if we weren't badly deceiving ourselves, then we could be happy with that, and why should we be deceiving ourselves so badly with someone if he came from the same town and we'd known him forever and his parents had a shop around the corner or they cut our grandfather's hair or sat behind the counter in the savings bank. But it still didn't seem right, coming from him.

I even went to the shop; I wanted to see her once in

the flesh. He'd told me she still worked there one day a week, so as not to spend all her time bent over the books, and I could understand that. It must be nice, selling bread; it smelled good, so fresh and warm at the same time, it couldn't make you feel ill the way you'd feel ill spending all day in a butcher's shop with the pig's head in the window showing you the back of its pink neck, and people weren't so picky about bread, they knew what they wanted and that they needed it, it made them happy or at least pleased and you didn't hear that endlessly calculating "I'll take a quarter of a pound—no, make that one slice less" that made you crazy if you were the next in line. I even knew the shop, it was in the neighborhood where I'd grown up; it really was a very small place with a simple display window, in which the same basket of bread stood year in, year out; as a child, I'd believed it was real bread. These days the display was more pretentious; they were pushing a calorie-reduced whole-wheat product baked into a wreath shape and advertised as perfect for evenings round the grill. I saw a young, very ugly girl hanging around behind the counter and waited for Karin to come out from the back room before I went in. I didn't have the nerve to start up a conversation about bread, but I also didn't want to be out the door again in two seconds flat, so I bought as if I were catering for a party and let two women go ahead of me in queue, saying I was afraid I was going to take some time. As she worked she was quite unrushed but concentrated: professional, you could say, except that would be a bit much when applied to a bakery; she talked for a few moments with a good customer but wasn't overly friendly to her, it wasn't any artificial sales skill, just a natural way she had, something that comes of knowing people for years. She wore her hair pulled back into a knot; it looked a little lazy, but it went with her practicality and her white apron; you seemed to feel calmer in her presence. I wondered if she had any idea that for weeks her husband had been taking off my underwear and whispering declarations of love into my neck, that he systematically lied to her and cheated, that we'd met each other two days before in a cheap bed-and-breakfast that traveling salesmen used and that we already had our next rendezvous all set for tomorrow evening in F., in a luxury hotel at the fairgrounds, where we'd have a room from seven to ten p.m. with a French bed. She looked so imperturbable that I wavered between sympathy and envy; I didn't ask myself whether I ought to be afraid of her.

■ ■ ■

They were even talking about it at the bowling club yesterday. Brigitte asked if it made any sense for the police to be making such a public fuss about the whole event when they were obviously making no progress, and Monica was also shaking her head over the to-do caused by the accident, while Irene said, almost in a whisper, that it was all just horrible. Irene's brother had been hit by a car while she was still a child, since then he had been unable to move his left arm properly; we all knew this, so we kept quiet. The general consensus was that it must have been done by somebody just passing through, because it happened just short of the highway; it couldn't have been anyone who lived in town.

■ ■ ■

Daniela was watching me quite closely. She was the only one who noticed that I was changing the way I dressed; I had lost another ten pounds and was now down to almost the same weight I'd been when I was a young girl. I no longer wore dark pants and skirts, the high-necked blouses and dresses were now in the back of the wardrobe, replaced by a couple of light trouser suits in pale colors, or a classic black two-piece with a side-slit skirt and several narrow-cut dresses in clear colors with open necklines, so that they would work both for business and in the evenings. I wore wrap skirts and blouses, things that you could remove elegantly, and I had bought black underwear because that's what Michael liked best. I had always gone to the beauty parlor once a month; now my visits became more frequent, and I changed the way I did my makeup. I had them put a reddish rinse on my hair, and I looked altogether more worldly, perhaps to underline the difference between Karin and myself, although I was not conscious of this at the time; I only wanted to look exciting, because that's how I felt, and it also worked. Ernst in his obtuseness noticed none of this, and when he registered it because Daniela's remarks could no longer be ignored, he told her amicably that she should leave her mother in peace and it was really nice if she was feeling good about herself. I could have taken pleasure from that, but it annoyed me, it sounded as if he wanted to protect me from my adolescent daughter: Have pity on poor aging Mommy living out the last flush of her youth at the warehouse. Irmi didn't say anything, her eyes were getting steadily weaker, and I think she wouldn't have noticed a thing about me; all she did notice was my restlessness and she worried about my sleep. My menopause was awful too, she said sometimes, her voice full of sympathy.

It wasn't even that hard to escape quite often for a couple of hours. Ernst had never taken any interest in my job; I didn't take him with me to office parties, it wasn't how Hermann's successor did things, and he hardly knew one of my colleagues. In his place I'd have become suspicious a long time ago, but he never asked me any questions—not about evening classes and not about anniversary celebrations and not about company dinners; instead, however, Irmi and he now insisted more often that I be on time for dinner, and paid attention to what I ate. There was a lot of talk about iron and feeding the nerves; I was supposed to drink beer and swallow vitamin pills. On our evenings out with friends, it was the women who noticed the change in me; some of them made significant glances as they remarked how much weight I'd lost, how well my new haircut suited me, how I looked ten years younger than they did. But I think nobody believed me capable of what was actually going on, because I had never complained once in all these years, never flirted and never sighed. I had always come with Ernst and left with him, we hadn't had arguments in front of the others, we were rated a harmonious couple and people even envied us a little—Ernst still because he got his beautiful Margarethe, and me because he was so good-humored. He never corrected me, never interrupted me, he never made jokes at my expense, he still invariably stood up whenever I came into a room, and straightened a chair for me, he helped me into my coat and opened every door for me, he didn't moan and complain that I smoked and drank. The only divorce in our circle had been incomprehensible to me—not least because I thought Hilde hadn't done herself any good when she swapped men. But when you came right down to it, I just couldn't imagine what the two of them had been up to for almost a year, she and her Rainer, on the backseat of his middle-range car or in her mother-in-law's apartment while she was away at the spa in S. Today I understood better; what I didn't understand was how you could live that way for a whole year.

I became rash. One time he canceled a rendezvous because he had to inaugurate an open-air museum in N.; the mayor of the town suddenly discovered he had a conflicting appointment. I had never been to N., an insignificant flyspeck of a place less than half an hour's driving away; there was nothing of any interest there. As it was, we couldn't have spent much time together anyway, because it was a Saturday and Saturdays were naturally sacred family time, which only made me angrier. Daniela wanted to go to a school friend's birthday party, the people had a farm quite a way out of town, and so I said I'd drive her there and pick her up again and in the intervening time I'd visit an old friend who lived in a nearby village. I put on a dress he hadn't seen yet, it was a late-summer day and very hot; the dress fastened with buttons, was made of flowered silk with a deep décolleté and a matching jacket; underneath all I wore was a bustier; I felt myself to be irresistible as I got into the car, I wanted to overwhelm him. Daniela sat beside me and sulked; she hardly spoke a word during the whole journey. She mistrusted me, but she didn't know why. As she got out, I checked the time: the ceremonies in N. would have already started, if I hurried I might still be able to hear his speech.

Which is what happened. I left the car far away down the street, because the car park was full, and walked to the event in the blazing heat. The former large dairy farm had undergone an expensive restoration, the walls freshly plastered and whitewashed, the half-timbering exposed, there was an old pump by the entranceway, a fountain splashed in the inner courtyard where the people were packed together. Standing on a small podium were several men in good suits and a thin woman in a dark two-piece, and he was talking into a crackling microphone.

The success of our structural reforms, he was saying, can be read in this house, which is not just both an open-air museum and a museum of our local culture but will also become a meeting place. For our communities, a place that can make the identity of our little world, the history of this district, and the social development of N. and its surroundings visible to the eye and an example to be imitated. It is by no means self-evident, he said, at a time of the general rationalization and devaluation of federal structures such as we're going through right now, that a place like this can be brought to fruition, one that bodies forth not only the living history of this area but also the conditions essential for life in epochs long gone, so that one's powers of imagination grow as one contemplates all those who once labored hard in the sweat of their brows. It was roughly at this point that a couple of cows and a donkey grazing in a neighboring field decided to join in, which induced laughter and applause—clearly people had already had a drink or two—and he took a step backward and exchanged a few words with the others on the improvised podium. Finally he took hold of the microphone again and talked about the technological revolution in agriculture, the intensification of use of natural resources, but also the damage to our quality of life through mechanization and standardization, which must be registered in this realm most especially. Division of labor, he said, despite its universally acknowledged blessings, most particularly in regard to productivity, is a double-edged sword. For the family-based means of production, which despite its economic disadvantages maintained a human dimension, has been almost totally destroyed . . . In that moment he noticed me; I was standing right at the back on the edge of the crowd, but my dress was fluttering in the wind and I looked right at him, because I wanted to know if he was glad I was there. He stumbled for a moment, but perhaps the family-based means of production was the catchword that made him nervous, then he managed to find his way back into his ideas and talked about the old means of production that are on display here, about the fountain and the interior decoration of the rooms, which recreates the lives of a great farming family of the early nineteenth century, from the wooden cradle all the way to who knows what, but at least it wasn't the grave. Finally he thanked all the people who had supported the project, he also listed institutions, one of which was Ernst's savings bank, and then the museum director lectured us about the population structure of the area in the late eighteenth century and the relative percentage of women and children and stillbirths, and then the mayor of N., a fat man with a beard, talked about something, but I can't remember any of it. I was watching Michael the whole time as he stood beside the museum director and now and then whispered something in her ear, which made her pull faces that were both nervous and sometimes silly looking; once she even laughed quietly, but at the end they both applauded the mayor. The donkey was still kicking up a racket.

First I went back to the car to get my pocketbook; then I lit a cigarette and went over to the field. I always have hotel packets of lump sugar with me, I like using it to feed animals, and although there were a lot of families here with children, I seemed to be the only one armed with provisions. The donkey came trotting over at once. I doled out the occasional sugar lump, but I wanted to have something to do for as long as possible, because I wasn't at all sure that Michael approved of my being here. The animals calmed me down, in particular the huge eyes of the cows, which observed me neutrally. I wished passionately that I was seventeen again; if I were as old as Daniela, I thought, or just a little older, this scene would have an innocent charm, because everyone believes a young girl is entranced by ruminant beasts; it's somewhat laughable in a grown woman—you don't stand there by a trampled field in a silk dress making yourself loved with lumps of sugar. I gave the remainder of my sugar to a small boy standing next to me and powdered my nose one more time before I reconnoitered the territory. I had no idea where Michael had got to in the meantime. I came past a building that was called the "Big Barn," it was totally empty except for various coaches and light carriages, and in the "Big Dairy" I saw a cardboard sign on the wall pointing with an arrow to the exhibition hall, and I followed it and saw a buffet laid out and approximately thirty people standing around together, glass in hand. Michael was talking to the museum director and two older men; he saw me out the corner of his eye as I came in, and immediately glanced away again, so I took a glass of wine and studied the exhibition texts on boards on the walls, all about manure methodology, barley soup, and sorrel salad. I learned that quite often back then an entire family slept together in one bed and the servants on the bench by the fire, and that a beechwood table stood in the main room, with a hollow scooped down in its middle, out of which the family and the maids and menservants all spooned up their soup in the evening. Suddenly Michael was standing there beside me and asked What are you doing here, and I was so disconcerted that all I could do was reply stiffly that I was surely allowed to look at an exhibition even if he happened to be the person opening it. You look ravishing, he said quietly as we were standing in front of a caption board explicating the production of wheat and the distilling of brandy, and I touched his hand and said in ten minutes in the big barn, then I wandered over to another board and read everything about rye, its uses and preparation, nutritional value and assorted pests, and on yet another board I learned all about how to make cheese. I didn't look back as I left the dairy; I heard him joking with the museum director and said to myself that he was my husband, even if nobody else knew but me. When he came into the big barn, we were alone, in a warm twilight; it smelled of straw and leather and just a little of some cleaning product. The coaches were labeled, there was even a wedding coach, an oxcart and an open wooden trailer; people had simply collected everything here that nobody in the neighborhood had use for anymore. From time to time there was the sound of footsteps on the gravel paths, children were playing some distance further off; the entertainment was in full swing. I leaned against a carriage and waited for him and when he stood in front of me I kissed him and leaned close against him; I felt him go limp and give way; we lost ourselves in that kiss that went on and on; when I opened my eyes again his gaze was unfocused; outside, a group of people made its way round the barn and headed for the entrance. I took his hand and pulled him behind me over to a large black coach; I opened the door and sat down inside and said Come here and as he hesitated the steps came nearer, so that he had no choice but to slip in quickly beside me and close the door from the inside. I leaned against him and placed his hand on my breasts while I kissed him again; I wanted to drain him dry and make him powerless. I felt more powerful than I'd ever felt in my life, as the group came into the barn and a man started droning on about spring suspension and iron-rimmed wheels. There must have been several people, going by the voices, women too, who allowed themselves to be lectured at with amusement and made fun of the spokesman and all his pronouncements. They were standing not far from us as I began to unbutton my dress; I heard him next to me moan with excitement and maybe anxiety; the coach rocked a little and we held our breath; his hand lay in my lap and mine was on his chest. I felt his heart under it as it pounded, I felt his excitement and kept undressing him while a man's voice somewhere very close to us said: That's a very old model, the seats will certainly be made of leather and there's room for at least four people; the coach springs moved a little as someone sat on the coachman's box and Michael undid the hooks on my bustier and his breathing got louder; I held his legs still with my own so that we didn't slide off the seat; outside the voices were encouraging the coachman. We could actually get in and sit down, I heard another man say, and Michael froze next to me; I reached out my hand for the door latch and held it tight from inside and for a long moment everything was simultaneous—the excitement and the fear, my desire to protect us and at the same time to set us free; I was still able to think clearly, yet I didn't care about anything, I just didn't want to give up; I wanted to stay excited and powerful, I wanted to have sex with him here in the coach, at once, I wanted to conquer him. Michael's mouth was on my breast as a woman outside said I have absolutely no desire to get into this hovel on wheels, let's go back into the sun; the man got down off the coachman's box and the carriage was still shaking as we heard them all leave, until the gravel crunched again and then everything went completely still.

■ ■ ■

In a week Daniela will be back from her last class trip. A strange idea to go away after your final exams, but apparently it's better that way, at least the stress is over by then. Although school hasn't meant a thing to her for the last year; she almost got held back going into senior year and it was only the prospect of being able to leave here after school that got her to work a little. How often around five forty-five in the morning I have heard the key in the front door and her steps coming up the two flights of stairs, and past our bedroom, not particularly quietly and slow only because of tiredness. She would sit at the breakfast table with red-rimmed eyes, sullen and lifeless, as if she were making an admission to us, and that is exactly what it was: she came home in the early mornings only because I forced her to. Pocket money was irrelevant to her now, she didn't care if I was worried, but Irmi shouldn't think badly of her. I had threatened her that I would tell her grandmother everything, with details if necessary; and no matter how cold she was to me, she was devoted to Irmi and probably realized that Irmi wouldn't have had the strength to deal with the truth.

It wasn't that way with Ernst; she was accustomed to the fact that he worshiped her, it went without saying, and nothing could threaten it, but there she misestimated herself. Still Ernst had no idea of the actual changes in her life; in his utter guilelessness he said the girl should be able to enjoy herself, and if I became more insistent he looked at me wearily, even a little spitefully, and asked, And you of all people want to lay down the law to her?

■ ■ ■

After the afternoon in N., something changed. I became cold-blooded and more demanding at the same time; Michael was surprised at me and sometimes didn't know what to do. He hadn't realized, he said one evening, what a wild temperament was hidden inside me, what a volcano. I made wild little celebrations out of our meetings; I waited for him naked in a hotel room; I bought champagne, appeared in a semitransparent robe or wore nothing under my coat as I waited for him at Reception; I got myself a book on aphrodisiacs and tested everything out; once I left a little tape set to record, and played it at our next meeting while we were making love. I didn't want any weariness and I didn't want any more repetition; each time had to be not only in a different place, it had to be a different experience, a completely new memory; I wanted to leave him speechless and helpless with love; I loved it when he trembled with excitement. I questioned him about his earlier relationships and his most secret desires and urged him on to everything; I wanted to make myself as essential to him as he had already long been to me. I gave him a ring that he wore when we were together; he brought me underwear that I kept in the car; once he put a little chain on my ankle, made of gold, with a tiny lock; soon there was a whole case full of special little things that we loved and that excited us. I blindfolded him while I made love to him, and I aroused him to a hardness that he didn't know he could achieve. I enjoyed it when he hurt me, yet I kept control over it. My passion increased, but my mind never stopped working.

I wanted an end and a beginning. I wanted to leave Ernst and start a new life with Michael and my instincts told me we couldn't wait that long. My fantasy seemed inexhaustible to me, but one day his wife would be bound to notice something, and then it would no longer be under my direction, but subject to her reaction, her threats, her fears, or her unflinching strength. I didn't believe Michael was very strong. He had always kept having affairs, as he willingly admitted to me; none of it compared in any way to us, he said, brief superficial relationships, sometimes one-night stands, on a trip, a further education event, or simply as an adjunct of some social event that he attended without Karin. She had never noticed a thing; she wasn't inclined to be mistrustful, was also completely immersed in her responsibilities as a mother and the head of her own business, and finally she had never had need to worry. They had a good, untroubled family life, the only negative factor being that she was tied to L. He would have liked to make a career, and felt he could have been successful; he had studied theater arts and worked as dramaturge for the famous N; he rattled a lot about the miserable state of German theater and how easy, fundamentally, it would be to tackle this misery—one had only to go and see N's productions, which attracted wildly enthusiastic audiences, as well as the critics. I encouraged him to talk about this, not just because I deduced that Karin never did so; it really interested me, and given how gifted he was, why shouldn't he be able to dare a new beginning? He pushed the idea away, but I could tell from the way he half smiled in a hesitating way that it appealed to him. After all, my contacts are still more or less in place, he said; an old friend of his worked at a big theater in B. and perhaps could get him in there on a project, on an experimental basis, naturally, no guarantees. I now read the theater reviews more attentively, also the ones in the regionwide newspaper that we'd subscribed to at the office; I noted the names that cropped up repeatedly and I even arranged for our bowling club to go to the Shakespeare production that had just arrived on tour in L. It was a bleak evening with a lot of screaming and yelling and harsh, cackling laughter; the actors chased one another all over the stage, the racket erupted from every quarter, so that you could hardly understand the text. Sometimes there were clouds of smoke, and music droned out of the loudspeakers periodically, only to break off abruptly again, without my being able to work out why. It was deafening; despite that I found it boring, but it's true that my thoughts were elsewhere. Ernst moved restlessly in his seat next to mine, and when I asked, doubtless reprovingly, if he weren't enjoying himself, he said Yes I am, very much. Maybe just a little loud? At the interval Michael came over to our group in the jam-packed theater café and talked about the "enormous intensity" that Z could still summon up. Almost all of us held back from any criticism, only Freddy spoke up quite loudly to say that the whole thing was over his head and what he'd really like was a good draft Pils; he'd set aside time specially to read up on the play at home and he didn't recognize a thing in this; and besides, he wondered how with all this madness going on, the madness of the king was supposed to make any impression at all; that was the only reason he was staying, it interested him technically, you might say. While he was grandstanding like this, Michael stood behind my armchair, in which I was sitting with legs crossed, smoking a cigarette. All of a sudden I felt his fingers brush across the back of my neck, so that all the hairs on my body stood on end. I wanted more than anything to beg him to stop and not to stop, ever; I didn't know if it might not be the best thing for everything to blow up right then and there, as Ernst worked his way through the crowd bringing a glass of champagne for me, dragging his left leg a little as he looked round in search of me. Just as he discovered me, Michael pulled his hand back, nodded to him casually, and moved off to another group that greeted him with hellos. He didn't look round at me again, and for a short time I felt hollowed out and helpless, as if he'd left me, as if in removing his hand from my body and yielding to my husband he had taken some final decision. Of course I told myself it was only reasonable, there was nothing else he could have done, but I was conscious of my dependence on him as never before. Ernst asked if I wasn't feeling well, I tried to smile and shook my head, before swallowing the champagne at a gulp with trembling hands. Ernst said once again how much he was enjoying the production and had I noticed how brilliantly the Fool did his acrobatics. We don't have that sort of thing here, he said almost contentedly, someone has to come from H. to show us how it's done. I didn't say anything. I looked at Michael's back in its black jacket just a few yards away, I almost didn't care if Ernst noticed something. I wished the whole world would go to hell, I just prayed silently that Michael would turn round for one moment and look at me, but he didn't.

The next evening we wanted to meet in a hotel in F. I had rented a suite and I waited for him there, unsure whether he was coming; I had turned out the light and lit a candle, but after I had lain on the bed naked for a few minutes, I felt as if I were in a grave; the little flickering flame, the surrounding darkness, the distant noise of traffic . . . I got up and fetched a terry robe from the bathroom, put out the candle, switched on the bedside light, and took a beer from the mini-bar. The TV choices were a sports broadcast, the news, and a western, none of it for me, so I lay there and smoked and thought about what ought to happen. When he eventually came, I was cold to the marrow of my bones, but I didn't want him to see that; I went to meet him tenderly and tried to hide my fury, which only a moment before had been fear. We took a bath together and drank a bottle of champagne, and when we were lying in bed and everything was almost over, I cuddled up tight against him and talked about

Venice. I had got it into my head that that was where we ought to begin our new life; it would be about a twelve-hour drive, a little less at night. I was absolutely determined that our new life should begin at night, for us and nobody but us. I had saved some money; it could last for two or three years. Irmi and Ernst would live happily together and Daniela was already going her own way; I would take the car, my savings account passbook, and one or two suitcases. Karin would carry on as she had before, her sons were past the most difficult age; we would start afresh in B. or someplace else; all that was required was that he decide. For weeks I had been carrying a brochure for a hotel in Venice around in my pocketbook; now in late fall there were almost no tourists there, we'd have the city virtually to ourselves. I repeated to him softly everything he had whispered in my ear in the previous weeks, all the avowals and promises, the complaints about his daily life, the ecstasy of our hearts, and our bodies. Finally I went to the bathroom and got dressed. As I stood in the door, my bag in my hand, he leaped out of bed and held me back; we'll do it the way you want, he said, and I lay down with him again.

It would be Wednesday night. I no longer know why this Wednesday; it was an ordinary day, but then it was also supposed to be; I didn't need sorcery, simply a clear head for planning things. I bought a new traveling coat of light poplin with a soft sheen and a removable wool lining, new shoes, two dresses, underwear, and a suit; also a suitcase lined in an unflashy pattern on dark red material. I wanted to take as little as possible out of the house and I wanted my new life to begin really new. I removed only a handful of things that I was particularly attached to from my side of the wardrobe to take them to the cleaners in advance. I took two favorite books, a photo of my parents, who'd both died years before; that was all. I mentally prepared a letter to Ernst, to which I would also add my wedding ring; that, it seemed to me, was my duty; he must after all be the first to know that his wife had left. At some point I would write to Irmi; she would understand at once, or maybe not at all—it was her son and her grandchild that I was leaving and with all mutual affection and respect, that must be more than she could condone.

I drafted the letter to Ernst in the office. It was an awkward document, more professional than personal, which may have had something to do with the atmosphere there. But I didn't want to be sitting at the kitchen table scribbling something in haste in the middle of the night, although what I did finally get down on paper may have been even more comfortless than a few lines written in a state of emotional tumult. It was something like a receipt without any numbers on it, but no matter how I tried, nothing better came out. I didn't want to make any confessions to him; the nature of our life must also have been clear to him, but unlike me he had been content with it. He was ahead by more than twenty years of happiness compared to me, but I didn't want to write that either; he wouldn't want to know what my plans were, and it was also nothing to do with him. Daniela didn't need me anymore—if she had ever needed me; I didn't have to worry about her upbringing, since no seventeen-year-old allowed herself to be brought up anymore, and anyway, Irmi was there to provide security and assurance. I tried to summon up the memory of some good times, so that I could say something comforting, but nothing special came to my mind, and I could hardly talk about some merry party at the bowling club. So all I added was that with regard to the divorce I would, within a reasonable period of time—I couldn't find a way to get round this formula, even though I knew that no such reasonable period of time could be measured— have a lawyer get in touch with him. I did tell him I was going away with Michael, for at least he deserved to know that, but I didn't say how long our relationship had been going on, and it wasn't really that long anyway. But he shouldn't be surprised by the news that Michael had left the town too. And it was up to him whether he said I was ill when the office rang up, and whom he told when, and what he would say to everyone; he should be absolutely free to say I'd gone mad or he'd suspected something like this for a long time or we'd talked about it again and again, but I was simply not to be stopped. How to end the letter made me rack my brains; finally I decided on "my warmest good wishes for all three of you," which was in any case the truth. I shredded the drafts of the letter and flushed them down the toilet. Then I took my few personal belongings out of my desk, my perfume, my comb, an address book, tampons, and a spare blouse; I left the hand cream where it was.

■ ■ ■

The woman who ran the gas station couldn't calm down. Imagine, she said, as soon as I came through the door, the Criminal Division were here! We were alone, it was already after eight p.m., so she took her time telling the whole story of the visit from the official on duty—the Commissar, as she intoned, looking important. He was apparently quite young and evidently very ambitious; he was laying everything on catching the perpetrator, and because he didn't have any other leads, he was checking all car washes in L. and the immediate vicinity. No car that had had a superficial wash, he told her, could withstand a full forensic criminal examination—it was a matter of skin fragments, threads of cloth, particles of earth—but he added that the perpetrator's first impulse would certainly have been to clean the car of all possible traces. I don't know, she said, when I think about it, you know, what happened—either the person was so cold-blooded that they'll never catch him, or he himself was shocked and dazed, and in that case they should already have found him, if he's from L., wouldn't you think? But if he isn't from here, but from F. or even M., say, they've got no chance, at least not now, after almost a week. Even I can't remember anymore who was here that evening; it was Wednesday, the Commissar said, but I had no idea anything had happened, so why would I have been paying attention? I have a lot of regular customers, but look, some of them can also be on holiday or on a business trip, and if someone's here all the time, one doesn't pay attention to the date, right? You, for example, God knows you're here a lot, but were you here last Wednesday and more specifically, were you here between eight-thirty and sometime later?—of course there are the day's records, which tell you how often the car wash got used. But who used it I have no way of knowing, unless the customer has an account with me, and there were only two of those customers that evening; he will naturally have found them soon enough, but I ask myself, if I've just run over someone and killed him and still have the brains to take the car to the car wash, then I'm not going to turn round and put it on my charge account, right? I could only signal my agreement by nodding at regular intervals; it was an exciting day for her and she was enjoying reporting on it almost as much, and wouldn't allow herself to be prevented from telling all her good customers about it for weeks afterward. Not that much else went on in L.

■ ■ ■

As I drove that night to the gas station, it still belonged to old Schustermann, who of course was not there. A pimply young man served me; I think he was the son of the lady who brought our newspapers, but he didn't recognize me, and we didn't exchange a personal word about anything. I drove the car through the car wash and filled up the tank, bought a chocolate soda to stay awake, two bottles of mineral water, some fruit and cigarettes and a map of Italy; I also had a coffee. I was totally calm and totally sober; everything had gone the way it was supposed to. Daniela and Irmi were sound asleep upstairs and Ernst lay there the way he always did, his arm across the bedspread, his breath rasping softly, as I got carefully out of bed and went downstairs, my suit over my arm. I dressed in the kitchen, took the letter for Ernst out of my pocketbook, and propped it up against the coffee machine. For years now he was the first to get up, because Irmi's medications made her sleep later. The overhead light was rather dim; now, in the middle of the night, the room looked a little shabby. We had always talked about getting it redone, but in the end it foundered on Irmi, who said she really got on best with the things she was used to. She didn't trust indirect lighting, dishwashers, or a new stove, and because this is where she spent most of her time, and because she still did the cooking for us, her opinion carried the day. So the wall cupboards were the same as were there at the beginning of our marriage, and the corner seat arrived shortly thereafter; only the table was a recent acquisition, because it had a surface you could wipe off. As always, the salt and pepper set was in the middle, next to it the plastic dispenser for artificial sweetener and a toothpick holder, which nobody ever used. In the sink a pot was still soaking, because the goulash had caught a little and I thought I would scrub it out and clean it, but decided against it; even the noise of the boiler might wake someone. Instead of that, I put the clean glasses back in the cabinet and hung and folded the dishcloth over the tap; I emptied the ashtray—we had gone to bed around eleven p.m. after we'd played Skat with Irmi; Ernst and I had lost and paid three marks to the Skat bank, which we all used once a year to go on an excursion together; we had drunk beer and I had smoked. Now the ashes were cold and the butts stank; I threw them into the garbage can to join the remains of the goulash and Daniela's yogurt carton. It was one-thirty a.m.; I had lain awake, without a conscious thought in my head, I had just lain there, watching Ernst sleep, and the alarm clock with its illuminated numbers. I didn't want to wait in the kitchen until finally it was time. The clock in here was never accurate, but Irmi felt that wasn't the point, a kitchen clock was only there to make you feel comfortable and at home, and she was probably right. The face was decorated with a pattern of onions; it was a cheap thing, most likely made of plastic, and nobody knew how it had gotten here. I had the impulse to take the clock off the wall and throw it away, but I didn't do it; none of it had anything to do with me anymore, not the cushion on the kitchen bench, the bluish-white dishes and the coffee mugs on their hooks above the sink, the egg timer in the shape of a rooster, and the banged-up bucket in which we collected kitchen scraps for the compost. Even the painting of little flowers that Daniela had made for Irmi's seventieth birthday and that hung in a frame over the corner seat meant nothing to me anymore. But I took a dishcloth from the rack and stuck it in my purse, then I switched out the light and crossed the dark hall, to the front door, which I opened quietly and closed behind me; I didn't take out the garbage. In the garage I switched on the light and looked around one more time; the open shelves on the wall, along with all sorts of odds and ends, still held things I'd brought with me from my parents' house but never carried over the threshold into my home with Irmi and Ernst. I saw the mirror lying there that had gone with me to the sanatorium; it was wrapped in paper, but part of the gilded frame shone out of it. The glass was almost blank, and covered in dust, with black streaks over it, but the frame glistened again immediately, as I rubbed it with my index finger to remove the thin layer of dirt. I laid it on the backseat and drove away, leaving the garage door open to avoid any unnecessary noise.

We had arranged to meet at three a.m. at the highway entrance outside F., where there was a small parking lot. Michael would take a taxi; he lived in the middle of town, and there was always a car waiting at the Three Kaisers Hotel. It was a little after two a.m. when I pulled in; I had stayed at the gas station as long as I could and even bought a magazine, but I couldn't concentrate. I didn't expect him to be any earlier than the prearranged time; nevertheless I watched the occasional sets of lights that drove past me or directly toward where I was parked. I was in no way anxious; I had never been a fearful person; it would just get hard to have to wait almost an hour. It wasn't especially warm, but I rolled down the window anyway as I smoked; now and again I glanced into the rearview mirror and looked at my face; I watched my composure gradually drop away. I did another check to be sure I had brought all the necessary papers; everything was there. I'd even thought to get lire, and the brochure for the hotel where I had booked us a room for a week was next to my savings book in my purse. I had taken the house key with me without thinking; I would throw it away somewhere. I turned on the parking lights; perhaps the taxi driver didn't know where exactly he should stop, when Michael said "to the little parking lay-by just before the highway, right behind the big gas station." It was only two-fifteen a.m. I hadn't doubted his decision, but I did know my decisiveness would have to be sufficient to cover us both. It was something subservient in him, although I knew he could act and even lead, but he sought out his opportunities, or rather his opportunities found him; he also just liked to let things happen when he didn't want to be disturbed. His restlessness was more a part of his psychological makeup; L. was too small for him and bored him, and the little excitements he organized for himself here couldn't satisfy him. My energy had made an impression on him, as had my uninhibitedness, and I had swept us both into a feeling that we could live all over again. The last twenty years unfolded in front of me like a bleached-out map; I could find paths on it that I had walked a thousand times and yet had hardly a single visible contour; I could have made a list of the sentences I'd said or heard again and again: Sleep well! or Does it taste good? or Is Daniela in bed yet? or Have you thought about Irmi's birthday? or Are we taking the car or going on foot? or Did you get the things from the dry cleaner? or Where are the aspirin? or Have you seen my key? or Is the coffee finished? or Did you lock up downstairs? or Are the eggs still fresh? or I think I'll keep reading for a bit, or This recliner is God's gift! or We'll never be this young again! or The rolls from Maier-Brühl are absolutely the best! or Now where's the TV guide again? or Ill weeds grow apace! or Shouldn't you lose a little weight? or Men have nothing to say about this, or Excuse me? or Raise your glasses! or I don't feel so well, I think I must be getting my period, or Freddy wants to know if we'll come to a cookout on Saturday, or Let's hope this rain stops soon, or I really must call Aunt Gisela, or We're not having any real summer this year, or Customers are much more sophisticated than they used to be, or My God, I'm exhausted! or Come on, Irmi, just one more little drink! or I don't know, shoes used to last longer, or I've been saying this for the last fifty years! or Won't we need gas soon? or Food and drink keep body and soul together, or I think I'd like the window closed, or Carrots are good for your eyes, or Don't shit in your own hat, or You were the most beautiful there, as usual! or That's just not true,

Ernst! or If it itches, scratch it! or Daniela doesn't have many friends, or Apples don't have a real taste anymore, or Cheers! or It's so nice we have the garden! or This milk carton always drips! or To us! or I can't stand this heat, or You're smoking a lot, or The rich get richer, or Irmi really is beginning to get old, or We're drinking her out of house and home! or This coat will last one more winter, or The garden gate is sticking again, or The little people always get it in the neck, or What a day, isn't it beautiful! or Did you remember the dog food? There weren't many unfriendly sentences in this catalogue, lots of friendly concern, lots of good will, lots of good cheer, though none of that was mine, not much worry, not much anger, not much surprise; as sentences, they were like oar strokes, regular, always on the same beat, always pulling in the same direction: we're rowing across the sea, the sea, we're rowing across the sea now. But I was no longer rowing along with them.

I had never wanted to get a divorce until I met Michael. Once, while we were still on our honeymoon, I stood on a balcony in the mountains and thought: You could throw yourself off here. It was a wooden balcony with a railing up to my waist, and of course it had baskets of geraniums hanging down in front of it, but I could have done it without any problem, if maybe inelegantly. It was on the fourth or fifth floor, a quite large hotel, correctly called the Alpview; a glorious panorama that took in the mountains almost ten thousand feet high and below, way below, at the foot of the precipice, a stony stream; that's where I would have landed, in the ice-cold water, though I wouldn't have felt a thing; it would have literally been a dead certainty. Ernst and I had had dinner and then sat at the bar with some people from the Ruhr; soon things got quite merry and I drank a lot. I went upstairs alone, saying to Ernst I would be down again in a moment; but he wasn't at all bothered, he was completely in his element. Much as he loved me, he would have felt a little uneasy to be alone with me from morning to night, without his friends and the club, without his usual surroundings and Irmi; neither of us had thought through what a honeymoon involves. We went to the Alps because the seaside would have been too hot for me, and Ernst wanted a holiday somewhere he could speak German. Now we were looking at the practically ten-thousand-foot peaks, green almost all the way up, with patches of remaining snow on the summits. Ernst of course couldn't go up there, nor did I want to go exploring by myself; so quite often we sat under a sun umbrella on the hotel terrace and there weren't enough of us to play Skat. In the evenings I changed for dinner and received admiring glances, but I was always just a little too elegant, and because it was whispered about that we were on our honeymoon, nobody came to sit at our table, as they didn't want to disturb the newlyweds. So we ate our way through three courses, twice a day; in the afternoons I went swimming in the open-air pool while Ernst slept in the hotel or read the newspaper, and then it was already time for dinner again in the small paneled dining room. It was a week before this group from the Ruhr arrived, somewhat older than us, outgoing people, whom Ernst got to know while I was off swimming, for they also sat on the terrace, drinking beer and playing cards and quite naturally invited the apparent loner to join them. When we came down together in the evening to dinner, there was a big Hello and I ended up drinking too much and it made me sad. As I stood on the balcony, a little unsteadily, I was looking into absolute darkness; the only glint of light came from the stream far below. I had successfully forbidden myself to think about Philip, yet now I realized he must be deep in preparations for his own wedding, but he wouldn't go to the Alps, more likely to Nice or Venice, and he wouldn't be going with a crippled club regular who took the newspaper to the toilet with him, he'd be going with a banker's daughter who spoke fluent French and had a hairdresser who came to her room. I thought I could have been in Liane Westerhoff's place if I hadn't been so naïve, if in my misery I hadn't fled like a dormouse. I couldn't believe he had never been serious; I thought of his letters, and I regretted having burned them; I would have liked to have read them now to prove to myself that it hadn't been his decision to leave me—of course he had had to marry money to save the overmortgaged family property, of course his mother had put pressure on him, of course he loved me still. I pictured myself packing my suitcase and disappearing the following morning back to L., where I would tell him quite simply that it still wasn't too late; I saw his face in front of me, full of happiness, it would be a deliverance. I went back into the bedroom and pulled my empty suitcase out from under the bed, but as I did so I banged my head on the end of the bed and suddenly I was sitting on the carpet, weeping; I had never been so unhappy in my life: I couldn't go back, I was absolutely drunk, and in my drunkenness I knew that there was nothing more to be done. I had made my bed and now I would have to lie in it: I would spend my life with Ernst, even if we never went to the Alps again; I would never see Philip again and he would never know anything more about me than what he'd learned from the announcement that I'd placed in the *Courier*. I stumbled back onto the balcony, leaned into the geraniums, and looked down until I got dizzy; it would last a second, it would look like an accident, albeit a rather clumsy one; it didn't require much courage, but more than I had.

In the bathroom I washed my face with a lot of cold water and put on a little makeup, then went downstairs very slowly and sat tight next to Ernst, who naturally put his arm around me as he carried on telling his story; I knew the story already, it was the one about his colleague who had booked a bus ticket to Paris and then went to Bulgaria by accident; it was a long story, from L. to Bulgaria, almost as long as this evening itself, but not as long as our marriage, which would, I thought from that time on, go on and on and on forever.

It was only a quarter to three and yet I was already

nervous. Only now did I picture how he would slip out of there, the way I had an hour before. He had told me that Karin often slept alone, in her room, when he came home late and she was getting up early next morning because of the children and because it was her habit; the baker's daughter and the man of the theater, you learned to adapt in daily life. I wondered when they made love; we'd never talked about it, of course. I couldn't imagine when they got together at all, because the daytime was impossible for Karin, on weekends the children were in the house, and at night they slept mostly apart. They didn't have a honeymoon at all, because Karin didn't want to travel anymore since her pregnancy was already quite advanced, and perhaps that made a lot of things easier; I didn't know what conversation with Karin consisted of if it wasn't about the business or the family; she didn't look as if she went in for painting watercolors, nor tennis; maybe, if anything at all, she went in for minigolf, but that seemed unlikely for Michael. They had a few years less than Ernst and I had, but that didn't change anything; after three years, at whatever level things were going well, was going to be as good as they got. You couldn't compare it with us; for Karin, Michael was apparently like some built-in cupboard; whatever didn't fit into her life was made to fit, but her life itself was already there; there were the house, the business, and L., there were her parents and grandparents, the children and later grandchildren to come, all solid, practical people, who accepted whatever they couldn't influence the way they accepted the weather.

For me, everything was beginning with Michael; I took almost nothing with me and I had no strategy. I'd planned this night cold-bloodedly, but I felt like the young girl in the allée, like the woman in the juddering car, I felt entirely and absolutely myself.

Now bells rang out over the town. I had determined not to feel any concern before half past three; all sorts of idiotic accidents could happen, perhaps there was no taxi waiting in front of the hotel this one time, and L. was so small; obviously you wouldn't ring the bell until someone woke up, you'd wait till the night taxi came back; sometimes someone wanted to be driven to F., which could take an hour, and Michael wouldn't have ordered a taxi in advance, because if anyone called back to check that Mr. Schäfer really did want a car waiting at the Three Kaisers Hotel at quarter to three in the morning, it could cause a catastrophe.

But what was a catastrophe anyway, if you wanted to leave your wife and children in the dead of night? I had told him about my letter, to encourage him; I'd noticed I had frightened him a little, maybe even shocked him; he had asked if I didn't want to talk the whole thing through with Ernst at least one time. It was pointless, I said; it wouldn't change anything now, I would only say more than was necessary and make Ernst even sadder; he would want to know specific details, and these would stick in his head; perhaps he would ask me to stay, and everything would be even harder for him because I wouldn't let myself be persuaded. I had made my decision; why should I torture him with the fact that nothing in the world he could say or do would stop me?

■ ■ ■

Two days later the newspaper said that the police now had a new theory. "Premeditation can no longer be ruled out." The dead man, so it said, had maintained contacts "in the red-light district," insofar as anything in L. could be so described. The circumstances of the incident—a bypass road on the edge of town, nightfall, no oncoming traffic—opened up the possibility that it was not a matter of a hit-and-run accident. In particular, previously established evidence pointed to intent: the victim had certainly been run down at high speed, no braking track marks had been found. If there was no assumption that this was the result of total drunkenness—for which there were no indications, the evidence of the tire tracks on the contrary gave clear evidence of perfect mastery of the vehicle—then how could one explain how a casual pedestrian could be hit head-on by a car right under the glare of a powerful traffic light? Which meant premeditation had to be a basis for one's calculations.

■ ■ ■

Now it was a quarter past three. The ashtray was full; I sucked a strong peppermint, powdered my nose once again, and awkwardly reapplied my lipstick. A screech owl hooted. The parking lot was faintly illuminated, and I could see across it quite well, but it was certainly too far for him to walk, particularly with a suitcase. We'd had no time to talk about such details, but I assumed that he, like me, had packed only the essentials; perhaps only an overnight bag that was kept in the office in case of need. I didn't even know if he had ever been to Venice, perhaps he thought my idea was simply silly and had been too tactful to say so? But that wouldn't stop him from coming; he knew he could talk me round, I would go with him to Helsinki too, or Warsaw. If he'd ever visited us at home, I would have showed him on the globe all the places I'd been: in M. and F., in the south of Spain and Majorca, in Copenhagen (on a bowling tour) and Budapest (another bowling tour), in the Black Forest, in London (bowling tour) and in Prague, and the Alps. We had always gone back to the same places, because Irmi felt better when she was in a place she knew; Ernst was the same, and I didn't mind really one way or the other. Daniela was always difficult and undemanding at one and the same time; you could never know what gave her pleasure; one time it could be a cow in a field and next time it could be Carnaby Street, and mostly it was Carnaby Street in a field and vice versa. On the globe the dots I knew made a cluster with very little distance between them, but that didn't matter to me. Not much mattered to me. I didn't know which dots Michael could have pointed out to me, and what pattern they would have made: had he already been in Paris? Must have! London, New York, Rome, Vienna? I didn't know but I assumed so; maybe he'd even been to Australia, maybe as a young man he'd been around the world. I imagined him in Belgium, somewhere on a small station. Had he had a moustache? Had he been in India, where so many students went now, had he been interested by the poverty, the transmigration of souls, the opium? I knew so little about him. I hadn't even brought any photos of me when I left; in the oak chest in the hall there was a cardboard box in which I'd saved everything, pictures of my mother as a girl and baby pictures of me, then later engagement and wedding pictures and finally Daniela when she was born. Then there were family snapshots, well meant at the time yet the results were unkind: people with cake in their mouths or clutching a sausage, with a smear of sun cream on their noses or asleep in the shade, people washing cars or changing diapers or baking cakes. Some of them were mementos of birthdays or special occasions, but none of them were as formal and dignified as the photos of my mother still were, leaning against a chest of drawers in her best suit or on a bank in a garden under the Virginia creeper, with my father when they got engaged, outside the church and then on their silver wedding.

It was almost half past three now and I couldn't

imagine how he had looked when he was a little boy; maybe he would at least bring a similar carton with him, of the kind everyone should have: with your first shoes or your milk teeth, the most important pictures, letters from your first love, your first savings book, perhaps your horoscope. I had forgotten or lost so much, destroyed some, and failed to value most of it enough to keep it safe.

The last twenty years seemed a kind of bleached-out approximation, something that had happened without me. I had never spent a day and a night in bed with a man, with nothing else on the brain except talking and making love. I had never sat on a kitchen stool, my mouth kissed raw, a glass of wine in my hand, looking at a plate of soup I couldn't eat because I was sick with love. I had never danced a waltz with a man in a living room, never just parked by the side of the road to disappear with him into a forest, never bought a summer dress and taken it off in the sunshine while he watched. I had never traveled with a man in a sleeping compartment and drunk champagne with him, I had never shown a man my diary, never gone swimming with a man, never spent Christmas alone with a man, or gone to a late-night bar, never been alone with one at the beach, naked in the grass, never gone to sleep in his arms under the open sky, I had never written a real love letter, never given a man all my money, I'd never taken the subway with a man I loved, or a taxi, never had him translate a menu for me, never eaten prawns with him, never made love without having to check the time. And now it was just after three-thirty in the morning.

■ ■ ■

I still remember exactly what raced through my head in those critical seconds; I saw my previous life and what was going to come now, I could tally exactly the causes for my hatred, all planted vertically like an iron fence; I was collected and fully aware; nothing would be more dishonest than to say I was completely beside myself. I knew what I was doing; I knew precisely why, I didn't want things to be any other way, I didn't feel in any way pressured, although I only had a matter of seconds. I wasn't prepared; it's true I had sometimes imagined what it would be like to meet him by chance, alone and helpless, but never like that, the way it actually happened, in the rain and the darkness, alone on the street, and me in my car at seventy miles an hour, with no one beside me who could have stopped me. Fate had reached out her hand to me, it wouldn't happen again, but I only had one or two seconds.

■ ■ ■

I know how that time passed, but I no longer know how the time passed after three-thirty a.m. while I sat in the car and waited for him. It was a clear night; I saw a few stars in the sky that I still couldn't name, although we had named the Milky Way to each other not five weeks before; but he knew little more than I did, and by the end we were both showing off a bit with the Big Bear and the Little Bear, the Evening Star and Orion. I turned the interior light on and off, because I could no longer tell whether it was off or on. I counted the minutes on the clock, to calm myself down and give myself something to do, but it made me too wound up. I shivered a little, because I was cold; I walked a few paces from the car and froze when something ran across my foot; I wasn't prepared for Mother Nature. Efrem Zimbalist Jr. came into my mind, I could see his big head right in front of me, shaking severely as he slowly and pedantically intoned, "It is unclear why the woman was waiting in the parking lot by the highway at around three-thirty in the morning; she was apparently alone and left the car for reasons we cannot ascertain." I sat in the car again and rolled up the window and turned on the radio. An announcer with a soft voice and a strange Dutch-sounding singsong of an accent was still presenting listeners' requests—at this time of night! they must be mostly long-distance truckers, to go by the names, the greetings, and the songs: Rowdy says "hi" to Buddy with "On the Road Again," Helmut says "hi" to Siggy with "Even When I'm Gone, I Think of You." I had nothing against country music, but the endlessly repetitive rhythm made me depressed. I would have liked a glass of wine, but that was quite impossible; I smoked a few cigarettes and switched on the fan, which was drowned out by the radio. It was approximately quarter past four when I first thought that maybe he wasn't coming. I went through the details of our meeting like a schoolgirl: time, place, date—could there have been any misunderstanding? I pulled out my pocket diary and checked the date I recalled for our last meeting. But the sentences were a blur; I saw myself more clearly than I saw him, I heard myself speak, but not his answers. I remembered the look on his face as he pulled me down to him, I remembered his voice when he said, We'll do it the way you want, or was it some other phrase? But as we left the hotel together, heading toward our cars, we held each other tight once more and I whispered Wednesday at three and he said I'll be there, and there wasn't any mistake. There wasn't any possible mistake. The way we held each other tight, the way he lay with me and breathed, the way we'd melted into each other the previous night and all the nights before.

I remember exactly how I almost gave up. My whole body was trembling; I was more shattered than sad, more despairing than sad; I thought, There's been a misunderstanding. I would call him later, something must have come up, or he'd gone to the wrong meeting place, he was probably sitting completely confused on his suitcase in another parking lot. I drove back to the street and once all around L., there was another entrance to the highway and I drove up it slowly; there was no parking lot there and nobody standing anywhere but I thought he's probably had himself dropped off here, and then he walked home, maybe to his office first to leave the suit-case. It was after five o'clock as I was driving around in the dark, then I turned and headed home, what else could I do? I had to get through the hours until ten. Then he'd be in his office and I could call him there; that was only allowed in absolute emergencies, but now the last and most absolute emergency had arrived. The time between now and then seemed longer to me than all the time that had gone before; I had waited for three hours, alone and in the dark, but now I was already counting the minutes until I would be delivered. I heard him on the telephone laughing and saying Sweetheart what did you do to yourself, I heard him whispering tenderly, I saw myself swooning with the receiver at my ear, I heard myself cursing myself, I saw us both smiling already about this ghastly night and how unnecessary it had been. I heard myself reporting on how I'd waited out the hours, I knew how hard it would be to tell him even the half of what I had hoped and what had gone through my mind. And I knew it would be impossible to sketch out for him the fears I'd had, but by then it wouldn't matter because it would all be over.

As I drove up to the house, I saw lights were on. It was not yet even half past five, and nobody got up that early. Perhaps Irmi had been unable to sleep, it happened sometimes because of her blood pressure; then she would sit in the kitchen, drink a rose hip tea, and read the TV magazine or knit a couple of rows. She wouldn't touch the letter, nor would Daniela, who would anyway be sleeping the sleep of teenagers, untroubled and deep. I parked carefully in the garage, pushed the map of Italy into my purse, and laid my coat on the backseat, over the mirror. I left my luggage in the car. The air smelled of machine oil and of iron, a little as it always did, and it was still almost pitch-dark as I walked the couple of steps to the front door. I turned the key slowly in the lock, suddenly feeling very tired, and said to myself Hold on, it'll be another twenty hours before you run off again, and I was glad I hadn't left anything in the office. It had been a soundless departure, it could be stretched out a little further, all I had to do was hold on until ten o'clock and I mustn't let anything show. I wouldn't have to make up any story for Irmi, she never asked me anything anyway that I wouldn't have wanted to answer; it would all be quite simple. I paused in the hall then quietly opened the kitchen door and there on the bench was Ernst.

■ ■ ■

I was very surprised, but not really shocked. I thought, I'm not afraid of you. As he stood there right in front of me he was a good two heads taller than I was, though I am not a short woman. He looked at me sharply, not exactly searchingly, perhaps just habitually attentive. Even before he introduced himself, I knew who he was; I calmly invited him in and offered him coffee, which he drank with milk and sugar, which impressed itself on me, because it seemed too comfortable for such a lean man. He was a little embarrassed and I didn't think to help him out; I waited and tried not to seem either hostile or unsure of myself; after all, I wasn't to know what he wanted. After half a minute of silence, he started to talk about it quite abruptly; I had certainly read or heard something about it. Read, I said, you could hardly miss it, the newspaper has something about it almost every day. So you did also, he said, looking restlessly around the room at Irmi's embroidered picture over the sofa table, the homely landscape in oils, the photos of my parents and the bowling club's twentieth-anniversary celebration, his pale eyes wandering, so you must have read of our theory that the dead man maintained contacts in the red-light district. That's what I read, I said, and couldn't suppress a smile, and that's what led you to me? In a way, he answered, and stared out of the window before he turned to me again. I take it that what I have to say to you will surprise and perhaps horrify you, but I have no alternative, it can't be put off any longer.

■ ■ ■

He had read the letter. I saw him sitting there, slightly hunched over, numb, in front of him the folded paper and the opened envelope. As he looked up at me, utterly thunderstruck but also as if dragged back out of every pain and every disappointment, the thought flashed through my head that I could dismiss the whole thing as madness, a whim, just more extravagant than my other whims, a sudden nocturnal excursion, a hormonal disturbance, something absurd that had already played itself out in the first gray of dawn. He didn't have much imagination, almost none apparently, but even he knew that there were truths that were only valid for an hour or two, that one was capable of things in the night that one not only rued in daylight but no longer even understood, even if it was only because he too got drunk once in a while and because the only times we got into a fight, it always happened in the middle of the night, when our nerves were shot, after too much to drink, after birthdays or major holidays that weren't as joyous as planned; at such times all it took was for one of us to say out of exhaustion Let's just go to sleep now, and next morning we looked at each other and had no idea what had been so important those hours ago that one had fought over it angrily half the night. It would have been a way out, and he would have half believed me and half wanted to believe me; I should have said Let's go back to bed, I can explain it all to you. I could have said it, but I didn't do it. In the moment when I fetched a glass of tap water and sat down beside him, as if for a great debate, and looked at him in silence, in that moment I lost the chance to make a nothing out of all this something, and make the catastrophe simply go away. I didn't do it; he asked why I had come back, and I said He didn't come. I didn't bother to lie, it wasn't what was important to me; I had neither the strength nor the presence of mind to think something up, and I thought Anyway, why should I? He was breathing heavily; I looked at him, as he tried to grasp what that meant; he didn't trust himself to ask. I will call him in a while, I said, we simply missed each other; it doesn't change anything. I shivered as I said this; I didn't know if I wanted to believe this myself, but I knew that the whole story with Michael was so infinitely more important to me than this man sitting crushed on the bench in this kitchen, and that I didn't want to belittle any of it. I also didn't want him to detect my anxiety which had now escalated to full-blown panic; it was nothing to do with him; I thought You've just got to hold on for an hour or two, then it's really over, you cannot just pull in your horns now. But it was no use. You want to tell me, he said, that you want to run away with a man, and he muddled up the rendezvous? He left the letter and the torn envelope lying there and went up the stairs with a heavy tread, leaving me just sitting there. I burned the letter in the sink, then I switched on the coffee machine and stayed sitting at the kitchen table until Irmi came downstairs.

The hours until ten o'clock went slowly, but I knew exactly how they passed, for I was determinedly busy. I went upstairs and showered and changed my clothes and straightened myself up; the night had vanished without a trace and at least my reflection in the mirror gave me something to hold on to. I had breakfast with Irmi and Daniela and said I had slept badly and was still desperately tired; Ernst joined us for ten minutes, only had a cup of coffee and left the house; Irmi must have thought we had had a row in the night, and that wasn't so far from the truth. The trip to Hermann's went the way it usually did, except that I kept checking the time and recalculating when I would be allowed to call him; after nine I could try, by ten he was sure to be there. In spite of everything I must have looked different, somehow, because Frau Voss looked at me oddly when I collected the mail from her; she asked if I wasn't feeling well, I said the same thing I'd said to Irmi, shut the door behind me, and sat down at my desk; I set the clock next to the telephone. I opened all the mail and wrote replies to everything that could be answered in writing; I was afraid to call anyone because my voice would have trembled. I forced myself not to chain-smoke, I also forced myself to drink a glass of water, just as I forced myself to go to the toilet before I called the first time; all these were minutes that I won the way a marathon runner wins the last three hundred yards. His secretary picked up and said immediately that he was not yet in the office; I asked when I could try again, she asked in reference to what. I wasn't prepared for this, the stupidest rote question in the book; I said I would call back, and so I had to wait until ten o'clock. I made it to a quarter-to, then the game repeated itself. I waited another half hour, and again she asked in reference to which matter I wished to speak to Michael. A private matter, I said helplessly. Sorry, she said, Mr. Schäfer is in a meeting, can I give him a message. Please call me back, I said, and gave my name and office number; a rage began to grow inside me because he was making me so despicable; last night we had wanted to start a new life together and today I was obliged to become a supplicant to the woman who guarded his outer office. I held out until the lunch break; that was my goal, and I succeeded, and then I had Frau Kalkenbruck on the phone again, who told me that she'd delivered the message, however Mr. Schäfer had only been in the office for a short while and now he was away having lunch. I asked her to pass him another message, it was very urgent, and I was reachable until six p.m.; she promised me she would and sounded almost kind; of course she couldn't know anything but perhaps she was touched by my voice, which must have sounded begging by now; perhaps she thought I needed a donation for a private theater or a ballet group. I didn't move from my desk, and if I had to leave my office for any brief period of time I took the phone off the hook so that there would be a busy signal. And somehow the time passed; some kind of darkness seemed to be rising inside me, something more powerful than this trembling that I couldn't control. I kept going through every individual detail, and once I called back again when I suddenly had the idea that Miss Kalkenbruck, the blond young lady at the ball where we met, was perhaps in love with him and simply intercepted anything private; but I couldn't get past her and her voice was friendly, even sympathetic as she said I reminded him specially one more time. It was as if I were under a spell, I couldn't think about anything, let alone do the accounts; I was hugely relieved that there were no meetings that day and nothing urgent to do; this form of relief was the only one I experienced in the numbness that pervaded me like a rigor, and slowly passed over into exhaustion. As I started to round up my things, I found I could hardly move my limbs anymore, they were so heavy; I couldn't find my comb and started mechanically opening all the drawers one after the other until I remembered that I'd stuck it in my bag twenty-four hours ago along with my perfume and the blouse and everything else except the hand cream. I could not believe that had been me, although I saw myself clearly in my red suit as, Love Personified but also quite unmoved, I emptied my desk. That was only yesterday evening, I whispered to myself out loud, but there was nothing to be retrieved; I wouldn't be packing my bag again. It's over, I wrote on a piece of paper, but even that didn't release anything inside me; I thought it would be sensible at least to cry at this point. But all I was, was bone-weary, as if I hadn't slept for weeks, and all the fantasies that had occupied me in the course of the day—to drive to his office, stand in front of his door, call his wife, wait in front of his house with my suitcase—all these fantasies had simply evaporated. There was nothing of me left over, not even hunger or thirst, not even the need to smoke, nothing left but exhaustion, not even fear of Ernst and everything at home, not even dread about what the future would bring. I looked into the mirror that hung next to the door of my office and saw an empty frame. I had left my coat in the car but I wasn't cold as I walked across the parking lot. I'd also forgotten to take my clock. I drove home very slowly, mechanical but precise, waiting for every light to turn green; twice I lost hold of the gearshift because there was no strength in my hand. Shops were just closing for the night, it was raining lightly, at a branch of Fühlmann Bakery a young girl came out of the door and turned in the twilight; everything in the world was in order, the woman who owned the bakery would be reunited with her husband at the dinner table, I was driving back to my family, I didn't even feel sick. The road home was long and could have been a thousand times longer, it wouldn't have changed a thing, the storm inside me had died, there was no more begging, no more hope, I was neither enraged nor grieving, I was nothing anymore, just a forsaken woman driving home. I didn't even have a bed of my own, but that would certainly solve itself; maybe Ernst had already anticipated this and prepared the sofa in the so-called office where our files were kept, a little room on the second floor that looked onto the street. Or perhaps we would sleep in our conjugal bed, the way we had for the last twenty years, it really didn't matter.

■ ■ ■

Naturally I played dumb at first. I let him wait a little before I asked, astonished but not confused, what all this was about. It's about your daughter, he said. Our information has brought us to a point where we cannot exclude the possibility that this was a normal hit-and-run, but we also simultaneously are pursuing the possibility that it was a deliberate act. I pretended not to be able to follow him. We believe, he continued, someone might have run over the man intentionally. You mean, someone who knew who he was? Yes, he said, that's what we think. I understand that now, I said, but what does it have to do with Daniela?

■ ■ ■

I saw him again three weeks later at a large event for all the clubs in the town. Ernst was to give a speech, which he had been working on all summer; I had read the manuscript several times and edited out the worst jokes long before the night itself. It was a major appearance for him. He had bought a new dark suit for the occasion and I knew he would make no allowances; I would have to go with him, even if only to dispel rumors that had never arisen in the first place. We had been so discreet that no one knew or even suspected anything, but that didn't change anything for Ernst; I must be at his side, and it really hardly troubled me. I was in such a state of apathy that I only began to tremble when I saw him at the other end of the reception room; of course he would be making the opening remarks, and it would perhaps be unavoidable that we would run into each other. And that's what happened, in the simplest way: I was walking past the rows of tables to the foyer, where the toilets were, and he was coming toward me with another man whom I didn't know. They were deep in conversation, and he glanced at me and acknowledged me with a nod, the way you acknowledge someone you know, but whose name you can't remember—so it was that simple, really, and as I sat on the john I was sorry I hadn't been able simply to throw up. I couldn't even do it now, although in my throat and chest and deep in my stomach, everything was heaving as if I were going to retch; I just couldn't make it happen. I would never have dreamed it was possible for two people who loved each other once to walk past each other like that, but now it didn't even surprise me; there was some kind of order in this even if I didn't understand it. When I came back to our table, Sabine pointed out to me that he'd come with his wife today—she must be keeping an eye on him! she said. And although I didn't ask about what she meant, she felt impelled to share with me everything she knew; that this Karin was naturally aware of all his affairs, but was sensible enough not to make any kind of drama out of it. They had a friend in common, to whom Karin often talked quite frankly; it was basically silly to exaggerate such things; that's how men were, he was a good father and aside from that a good husband too, and in ten years it would all be over anyway. I must admit, Sabine added, I couldn't do it, but it's amazing, and basically she's right. Of course she could make a scandal of it, but what would she gain from that? Only a war at home and no better man if it did come to a separation. He knows what he's got in her, fourteen branch bakeries and a lifelong certainty of no worries; he'd be a fool to push things to the limit. I said nothing; I was devoid of all feeling. All that was left was a body that spoke and washed and dressed itself, a body that worked and had a name. I took this body home; I was my own keeper, I fed myself and laid myself down to sleep and then I got up again.

Ernst, naturally, did not forgive me. Nor did he have any reason to, for I was not ready to show any remorse. Naturally I felt wretched, at the end, and no longer myself, but I felt so wretched that I couldn't even manage to say I'm sorry, and it would have been better if it had never happened. He had a wife in his house who was crawling on all fours like an animal because of another man, why should he have forgiven me? I was not in a position to strike Michael out of my life; I hadn't been able to strike Philip either, though it took me a very long time to understand this. I was in a state where I could imagine a life without Daniela, without Ernst, and even without Irmi, but I could not imagine my life without Philip and without Michael either; it had happened, nothing changed that; I would have had to lie and I didn't have the strength for it. I avoided situations where I could possibly run into him, I was just capable of that much forethought, and I also had no yearning to see him anymore; I didn't want to be ignored again, I had really gotten the point. At night I lay beside Ernst and waited in my hundred-horsepower Audi, smoked till the ashtray was full, and counted the minutes until he wasn't coming anymore. Ernst had taken my mirror out of the car; it didn't reappear and I didn't ask what had happened to it. Perhaps he assumed it had been a present from Michael. Daniela and Irmi crept around us and treated me like an invalid, but even Ernst received special care; an indefinable benevolence filled the house, reminding us constantly that something had fallen to pieces. I don't know if Ernst was in torment, but nonetheless I was glad that he didn't know any details; that made things easier for us both, although "we both" no longer existed. I breakfasted as I'd done every morning with Irmi, Ernst, and Daniela. I put milk in my coffee and marmalade on my roll, as I listened to the traffic reports, and drove punctually to the office. In the evenings we ate together as we always did, only there was nothing I could think of to say anymore, and so sometimes I drank too much. Ernst exercised a kind of sarcastic forbearance; he didn't reproach me, but kept watch on me like an enemy, and from time to time he found the opportunity to humiliate me in passing. He just left his underwear lying on the floor, so that I had to pick it up in case Irmi did it herself; he belched in front of me and waited to unbuckle his prosthesis in bed until I was already lying on the other side. He no longer asked if I was tired, but went to bed alone and read there for as long as he felt like it, every kind of magazine; sometimes I found sex magazines under the bed, which I hid away because of Irmi. When he wanted a beer, he just said Get me another bottle, as if it were a matter of course, and what had once been a customary act of affection was now a servitude. One morning I found the underwear I'd bought in the last months in the garbage can, with the coffee filter and an ashtray emptied on top and a couple of apple cores added to the mix. I wasn't even angry at him, it was a relief in a way, but I did ask myself when it would all come to an end. When we were in company his behavior was almost unaltered, he helped me into my coat and held the door open for me; no one seemed to notice anything, I was the only one who saw his glassy stare, I was the only one who saw him counting the glasses of wine I drank, and I was the only one who feared the journey home, while he sat next to me in silence and slammed the gearshift. Daniela, who was growing up so fast that it was eerie, sensed the shift in the balance of power and now only asked Ernst when she wanted something. In the evenings she went to a disco that had a bad reputation, but Ernst never refused her anything and if I expressed any doubts, he looked at me the way you would look at a dog that inexplicably has the power of speech. He started telling the kind of jokes again that I had told him he couldn't for years, he wallowed in stories that were risqué or just plain dumb, he reveled in the laughter of the men around him. His face changed, and sometimes he made remarks that stunned people, not just me; there was a recklessness in him that repelled me like some kind of skin disease. But he was universally loved; all everyone wanted from him was that he be the life and soul of the party, and he served everyone stories that amused and shocked them simultaneously. He put his arm round me when we were in company, and sometimes his hand slipped down and lay on my breast, so that I had to push it away or simply get up and move away, so as not to become a laughing-stock. On evenings like these I knew what was coming, that, to use his expression, my due date had come, and I didn't have the strength to defend myself, and indeed why should I? As long as I lived in the same house as him, as long as we were man and wife, as long as he didn't throw me out, I was in his debt. We never said a word while it was going on, and I never held him anymore as he rolled onto his side, he never touched me afterward either. None of it appeased him; nothing could appease him except, perhaps, time; and I had no more plans. Some-times I played with the idea of going alone to some unknown city, but it was only a passing thought and nothing came of it, not even a phone call to another company. I lay there and stared at the alarm clock; some-times I thought back to our honeymoon, and occasion-ally I would have been glad to know what he was remembering—perhaps the lively evening at the bar with the group from the Ruhr, perhaps our first, rather complicated night with the prosthesis and my inexperience. But I never asked him.

■ ■ ■

He was silent for quite a long time, and finally I asked again: What has all this got to do with my daughter? Our information, he said, tells us that your daughter was well acquainted with the deceased. We are investigating both the professional and the personal life of Mr. Willrodt to ascertain possible motives for this act. But how could Daniela help you with that, I asked, my voice still calm. Your daughter and Mr. Willrodt, he answered, knew each other well. Very well. I would know if that were the case, I said firmly. I don't follow the changes in my daughter's life from hour to hour, but I would certainly know about any close relationship. Your daughter is not yet of age? he asked. In a month, I said. But that doesn't alter the fact that I'm her mother, that she lives here in this house and still goes to school. She has been seen with Mr. Willrodt, he said neutrally, several times, also in the evening and the early hours of the morning. She often comes home late, I acknowledged, and began to betray a little confusion, and she loves to dance. She visited Mr. Willrodt at home, he said, and his employees have stated that the two of them had a relationship. Is that your daughter, he asked, going over to the wall where a photo of her hung, taken the previous summer—Daniela in a bikini on the beach on Grand Canary Island; she had given the picture to Ernst for his birthday. Yes, that's her, I said, introducing a note of consternation into my voice. Then there is no possible doubt, he said not looking at me directly. We found a whole series of photos in the dead man's apartment, which show your daughter. The photos—he paused for a moment—the photos are all studies in the nude. I don't believe it, I said with a trembling voice, I simply cannot conceive of it. I'll leave you an envelope, he said carefully, then you can see for yourself if you so choose. Your daughter is still away on a class trip? Yes, I said, until Wednesday. So they had already found that out. I would like to talk to her, he said, and gave me a card. Please tell her that she should call me at headquarters. But I still don't understand, I said when he was already on his feet, how the child can be of help to you. Your daughter may be able to give us information that we could obtain from no one else. We have to try all possibilities. In this milieu research is difficult to do, because almost everyone has something to hide. My daughter would also have something to hide, I thought, but she isn't bothering anymore. In that way she's like her mother.

■ ■ ■

I rocked with the tide. I never tried to ask Ernst for his forgiveness, and he never forgave me. But as time went on, it became too tiring for him to play the role of despiser; he kept up a certain negligence, he made the occasional nasty remark, but his natural tendency was toward good humor, and his character was stronger than his will. He had no more grounds for jealousy, and he knew that, and he also took no pleasure in breakfasting with misery, going to bed with it, sleeping with it, and going to parties. When we were alone, it was still difficult, but we were almost never alone, although Daniela quickly went her own way. She appeared at breakfast already with makeup on, wore very short skirts and tight little tops, but I didn't know what to make of it. I couldn't believe that a girl of sixteen could have the faintest idea of how a man would react to such a thing; now and again I read the childish little publications she hid in her clothes closet, articles about tongue-kissing and contraception and "your first great love," both simplistic and over the top, and I tried to remember how I had spent my time at the same age. When I talked about it with Renate, she laughed in my face. We were such innocent creatures, she said with absolute conviction, compared with girls today. Since the divorce her daughter lived at boarding school and only came home for the holidays. I expect you won't believe this, she said, but these girls are no longer children, they experiment far more than we did, and that's why they're much more self-assured. There's no point in worrying about them! She almost laughed my misgivings away, and what remained was mine to deal with. When I tried to speak to Daniela, she just looked at me stubbornly; maybe she was as helpless as I was, but the most I could get out of her was the assurance that she could take care of herself. I wondered what that could mean in a girl of her age, but I didn't ask, because I was afraid of what the answer might be. Sometimes she brought home friends from school, and their appearance comforted me; they all wore tight trousers and sweaters, mascara and eye shadow, but when I walked past Daniela's room I heard them talking about logarithms, English vocabulary, and "the totally adorable boy in 10B"; they were children, wanting to look like their pop idols. And finally I also knew that my authority had exhausted itself. Once, when Daniela was awake in the night, she found me alone in the kitchen with a bottle of red wine, hardly able to speak anymore. She heard Irmi and Ernst talking about my drinking, Irmi always with concern, Ernst initially nasty and then migrating to an awareness of his "responsibilities." That's how it was; under Dr. Lehmkuhl's care I managed to get a better hold on myself—that and, naturally, the threat of being shipped off to a clinic. An evening without alcohol was something I couldn't imagine; I drank toward the moment when I was just on my own, almost undisturbed by the others, in a pleasantly fuzzy state that would last until I fell into bed. It was a long time since I'd had to worry that I would turn aggressive or fall into despair; it was just that sometimes after the second bottle I had the urge to call Michael at home, and once I actually did it. I wasn't hoping for anything in particular, I wouldn't have known what to say, I just wanted to disturb the two of them, I wanted to show him that I was still here, and perhaps I also wanted to hear his voice. But I was out of luck, because after the phone had rung for a long time, she picked up and I immediately put down the receiver, heart pounding and in some idiotic way proud of myself, as if I'd passed some test of courage. I pictured how she would make him talk in the night, because she would certainly suspect something that was in fact correct—not that it was me, but perhaps someone else, the next one, or the one after that—I hoped he would lose his sleep while I grimly poured myself another glass.

During this time Renate was my only anchor. She told me stories about her two husbands—she improved her situation measurably with each divorce—she could mimic herself enchantingly and had such joie de vivre that she infected even me. I told her a great deal too, and a lot of things found their resolution simply because I was able to put them into words. Ernst didn't like our relationship; like many people who love to tell jokes, he actually had no sense of humor, and Renate's laugh made him nervous. Although she conducted herself extremely well to all outward appearances, she didn't give a hoot about good behavior. She wasn't afraid of anything anymore, all she wanted to do was find another husband, and so I accompanied her now and then to saloons and bars, where she couldn't really go on her own. There weren't many possibilities in L., so sometimes we drove all the way to F., even to places "for lonely hearts" with telephones on the tables and a revolving crystal ball above the dance floor. On evenings like these I stayed sober—not least because of the long drive home, but also so that Ernst couldn't say that Renate was leading me astray, and he had no idea about the rest. I told him I was visiting Renate at home, and it would never have occurred to him to spy on me; on the contrary he was happy that I wasn't bringing her back to our house. There were only two bars in L. that were in any way possible, in the two better hotels, and I could be certain I wouldn't meet anyone I knew in either of them. In the Three Kaisers we began by sitting on the high barstools, but in tight skirts it was too much of an effort, so later we changed seats and went to a corner where we could sit in deep armchairs with a view of everything that was going on while remaining almost invisible ourselves. When Renate was interested in someone, she always found a way to strike up a conversation with him; she was also not above asking for a cigarette, since good behavior was not her concern. I tell him I'm trying to give it up, she said, and that's something to talk about right there, and he feels good about helping me out of the mud. So the three of us would sit there, and I'd listen to stories about business trips and three-star restaurants and winter sports and brands of whiskey and Mexico or the USA; the only things that never came up were wives and children. When I felt a candidate was beyond the pale, I would ask him for a cigarette too; the rest was up to Renate. I have good instincts, she said, but you have no active involvement, so to speak, so you're more objective. And besides you're more afraid of disappointments, and that always keeps one alert. So when she was unsure and I asked for a cigarette, the evening often ended quite shortly afterward, but sometimes she also ignored my signal and stayed sitting until I said good-bye. Then I drove home alone and imagined how the story would continue; the exciting thing was that the next day I would hear what actually happened. Renate was merciless in her candor, even about herself, so I learned all about tactless remarks, catastrophes in bed, impotence due to too much liquor, and being thrown out at three o'clock in the morning with a ten-dollar bill for a taxi. There were also better nights, but nothing more long term ever came out of them—until that evening that was also a significant one for me.

It was in the Three Kaisers, we were sitting in our corner and watching the bar. A well-built man in his mid-fifties with a moustache had attracted Renate's attention and even I liked the look of him too. There was something peaceful about him, he seemed solid and yet not entirely at ease. He wasn't smoking, so the number with the cigarette was no good. We tried to think up another strategy, but the more clever ideas we came up with, the more awkward the whole thing seemed to me. He's not the type for tricks, I said, you'll only make a fool of yourself. So I'll tell him the truth, she said finally, stood up, and walked right over to him. I saw them exchange a few words and then the two of them came back together. Your friend, he said as he held out his hand and introduced himself, thought I looked lonely, and she's right. He was a real estate agent from M. who had set his sights on a big property here; the negotiations had broken down and so he was spending the evening here before driving back next day. Instead of tying up a contract, he said, I'm tying one on with a bottle of cognac, so it's really much better to have a glass of wine with you.

He was the first man who made immediate mention of a woman—namely his ex-wife—and that drew me to him right away. Renate's instincts had been right, he was lonely and a little sad, and he was impressed that Renate was simply pulling him out of it in her warmhearted, animated way. We were sitting together having a really good time when the door opened again—it was about midnight by now—and my daughter walked in.

She was wearing a little dress that I didn't recognize—either she had borrowed it or hidden it from me. It was covered in sequins and had a ridiculously low neck—ridiculous above all because she had almost no bosom. Along with this were extremely high heels and see-through black stockings. The man at her side was powerfully built and quite good-looking in a rough way; his suit was a little tight. He was tall and broad-shouldered and tanned, as if he'd come directly from Ibiza or a tanning salon. He was dark, his hair a little long and stringy, down to his collar; the artificial light in the hotel bar made his shirt glow white and emphasized his big teeth as he laughed. His arm round Daniela, he led her to the bar, where they sat down with their backs to us. I saw that he soon had a drink in front of him, and she a glass of champagne. They toasted each other and he put a hand on her thigh and pushed her dress up. It was a gesture that made me shudder, it looked in every way so routine, a self-evidently proprietary gesture that was just as self-evidently indifferent; the fact that it was a well-manicured, long-fingered hand and not a cattle dealer's paw only made the whole thing worse. He was wearing a ring with a stone in it, I could see even that from where I was sitting, and he took his hand off her thigh to run it into the hair at the back of her head; he shook her head a little, as if she were an animal, and she let him do it, laughed and closed her eyes. I didn't even think about the fact that she could have seen me; I was appalled and sick to my stomach, because there was no doubt about what I was seeing. That was my daughter in a hotel bar in the middle of the night in a shred of a dress with a man who was behaving like her pimp, and she was clearly quite at ease. She had put her hands on the bar and was playing with a lighter while he whispered something into her ear. Then she laughed, took another sip from her glass, stroked her dress back down a little, and then let her hand be pushed back up again. Renate noticed I had gone rigid, but didn't understand why; she hadn't seen the two of them come in. I said I had just realized that there was a piece of unpleasant business I had to sort out in the office next day, and she should please not worry about it. Nothing in the world could have made me stand up; I wanted to see how the scene would play out, and I wanted the evidence of my own eyes to overcome something I believed to be quite simply impossible. The man played with Daniela's little gold chain—a present from Irmi for her sixteenth birthday—and made a knot in it with his finger, so that he could move her neck forward and back. She pretended to resist, but let it happen and finally licked his forefinger, then he let go of the chain and put his hand on her thigh again. The bartender gave himself something to do elsewhere and the guests were all occupied; no one seemed to be observing the two of them, but their movements were also too small to be noticeable. I had the feeling that the man was also aware of this; he wouldn't take things so far as to cause a scandal, but he went right up to the limit. He pulled greedily but absentmindedly a couple of times on his cigarette, then let it fall into the ashtray, where it continued to smoke until the bartender took the ashtray away. He scraped his shoes along the legs of the barstool and ran his hand over her back; she lowered her head and sat quite still, her naked elbows held tight against her slim waist. She had another glass of champagne but she wasn't enjoying it, that was clear from her face, which I could watch quite clearly, sometimes in the mirror and sometimes in profile. While the man paid, she dug around in her purse and touched up her lipstick, then the two of them left; she teetered on her high heels, he had his hand round her waist, the doorman held open the door for them, and I heard an engine start outside. The night was clearly not over for them yet.

■ ■ ■

The photos are absolutely horrible. The most harmless of them shows Daniela lying on a bed with black sheets, her legs spread, holding a teddy bear in her lap. She's laughing, as if she's not quite in her right mind; there are plastic rings on her fingers and a gold chain around her waist, but otherwise she is completely naked. In another photo she's posing like a dog; she has a leather collar on, she's on her knees, the picture is being taken from behind, but she's turning her head back toward the camera and letting her tongue hang out. In lots of photos she's seen from behind, you can see the fine red-blond hair falling over her shoulders like a fringe; she lies on the black bed sometimes with her legs spread, sometimes closed; in one of them she's holding a stuffed frog tight in her behind and the frog is grinning at the camera. They're amateur photographs; you can see shadows where there shouldn't be any, even the skin of this young girl looks oddly patchy, as if the connecting tissue could no longer stand up to a flashlight. The pictures are careless, despite all the expenditure on scene setting and stuffed animals; if the naked girl were not Daniela, I would find them laughable, tasteless, maybe just inept and cheap. But it is my daughter who's there with toys between her legs, who's posing in the bathtub with rubber ducks on her breasts, who's licking the face of a teddy bear. It's my daughter Daniela who will turn eighteen in a month, and for whom there's almost nothing more I can do.

■ ■ ■

I heard the key in the lock in the mornings and her weary footsteps coming up the stairs; I saw the shadows under her eyes, but I didn't know what to do. When she said something once about moving out just before her final exams, I took her into her room; I said I knew about the man she was spending her nights with, and if she didn't want to lose her grandmother, it would be a good idea to go on posing as a schoolgirl for a while. She didn't ask how I knew, she walked past me into the bathroom and started running a bath, but I could tell from her attitude that the threat had worked. I was beside myself with pain and worry; we had never had a close relationship; we really didn't know each other—but the idea that my daughter, Daniela, had fallen into the hands of this pimp was making me half crazy. I talked about it with Renate, who was in seventh heaven and organizing her move to M.; she said casually: Then talk to him, and finally that seemed to me the most sensible thing to do. I didn't promise myself it would work, but I hoped that some kind of confrontation—the woman from the row house and the man from the underworld—might just lead to him pulling back. I thought that if I managed to appear narrow and bourgeois enough, then possibly he would lose his appetite for Daniela; perhaps he would recognize that her "bearing" was an error, that she belonged somewhere else, that it was only the yearning of an adolescent to leave her world just once, as a kind of test. Perhaps I could also intimidate him, if he could clearly see in me that I wouldn't tolerate it any longer, and that I would do something about it. None of it was wildly original. But I had seen the man. I didn't believe money would work.

■ ■ ■

Today she came back. She didn't pick up any news in the school dormitory in the Tyrol; there were certainly no German newspapers there, and even more certainly none from L., and apparently they didn't phone each other when they were apart for short periods—he would also most certainly have been hard to reach, as the owner of three discotheques and two topless bars. I had collected some articles about the incident and put them in her room in a sealed envelope that also contained a note I'd written. Dear Daniela, I'd said, in connection with the death of Mr. Willrodt, the head of Criminal Investigations—his card is in here—would like you to call him at headquarters. I hope you get over all this soon. Your mother, who loves you.

■ ■ ■

So I called him. It wasn't all that complicated to find out
which hangouts Willrodt liked to use, but it was difficult
simply to reach him on the telephone. I left my number
several times with no success; finally I flushed him out
one night around ten o'clock in a bar on the Fried-
richstrasse. I am Daniela's mother, I said without pream-
ble, and I would like to speak to you.

He didn't even pause for a second; it even seemed to
amuse him. That can be arranged, he said, do you want
to come and see me? I hadn't thought about where I
would like to meet him, but our house was obviously out
of the question, I didn't want to be seen with him in a
café, and I was also impelled by some element of curi-
osity. We settled on six o'clock the next day, and wearing
a navy-blue suit and a conservative silk shawl I got out
of the car in front of his house.

It was an apartment in an old building, like many in
L., particularly on the first floor, spacious and dark, with
a long hall and many doors opening off it. His body
almost filled the doorframe, and I could hardly recognize
his face; we did not shake hands. He said hello in a voice
that was amused, deep, and hoarse from smoking, and
led me into a room hung with pictures of seminaked
women in plastic frames, some of the figures partially
overpainted in harsh colors. A couch upholstered in light
brown corduroy, a glass coffee table, two low armchairs
facing it. Under the window was a drinks trolley with all

sorts of bottles on it, and although I would have loved a glass of red wine to steady my nerves, all I asked for was a glass of water. He poured himself a whiskey, sat down on the couch, and grinned at me; he seemed to be enjoying something and even slipped his shoes off; I saw white socks with grayish soles. You know my daughter Daniela, I said, and he kept grinning. I cannot sanction this relationship; you must know that she's still in high school, she has to prepare for final exams, and I hardly think that an involvement that takes up so much time, including in the evenings, can be reconciled with that. He stared at me unwaveringly with cold, pale blue eyes. His gaze inspected my body and then paused on the coral brooch I was wearing. He still didn't say a word, but I was prepared for that; I didn't want to speak to his conscience, for I was sure he didn't have one, I only wanted to be the narrow-minded bourgeois mother spoiling his fun. Daniela isn't good at Latin, I said, she needs to take remedial classes, and I'm sure you're aware that a good school-leaving certificate is worth more these days than a one-family house. I am appealing to your sense of responsibility not to confuse the child; this is the single most important period in anyone's life that Daniela is in right now, I'm sure you understand. He took a cigarette out of a shining metal container on the table, lit it, and still didn't seem inclined to say anything. You and I, I said almost guilelessly, have the best times of our lives behind us, for all intents and purposes, but the child has the future to think of. He looked at me more closely and seemed to be calculating my age; for the first time I really regretted that Daniela didn't physically resemble me in the least, maybe that would have spoiled his appetite. I had lost my looks in the last years; my hair had turned gray and was brittle because of all the coloring, and finally the consequences of all the smoking and drinking had declared themselves; I had some deep lines around my mouth and my chin was no longer taut. Having put on weight again I was now almost the little suburban mother I had never wanted to be. Still he was leaving me to talk. I am not here to threaten you, I said. But you should know that sexual relations with a minor are a crime, and if you do not break off your relationship with Daniela, I will have to take the appropriate steps. I had no doubt he understood me, he looked alert and cold and absolutely not stupid. His face seemed more worn than his body, which exuded power; he seemed utterly self-assured. Despite his intentionally casual attitude, you could feel a tension, as if he could leap up at any moment and do something completely unexpected. I heard my own voice as if it were coming from a distance, and hoped that it didn't betray the trembling that was running in waves through my body.

I waited for him finally to deign to reply. Eventually he leaned even further back into the couch, until he was lolling in it, crossed his legs, and smoked. Very pretty, your speech, he said, it really touched me, that whole mother and child number. A school-leaving certificate is certainly a fine thing, but you can see from me that it's possible to do very well without one. Daniela can learn all the Latin vocabulary she wants, it doesn't bother me. But if she has more fun doing other things, I can't help it, can I? Until then he had seemed almost uninvolved, but now he leaned forward and looked me straight in the eye. And I'm telling you, she has a lot of fun! Grinning, he leaned back into the couch again. And that's why your threats don't interest me. Daniela is about to attain her majority, and then no one can tell her what to do anymore. And if you interfere with us, you will get the shock of your life. Your little daughter learns things very fast—maybe more than she does in school. It will not enter her head to complain about me. On the contrary, she's learning a lot from me and I've not finished by a long way yet. Then he got to his feet. I thought I was going to vomit; I followed him along the dark hall to the front door. As I tried to pass him, he seized my elbow and whispered, You should be happy. Your daughter experiences things with me that women like you have only dreamed about.

This time Renate could still comfort me, as far as that was possible. She was almost sitting on her suitcases, packed and ready to go, when I rang her doorbell; the moving van was due next day and she would start her new life in M. I didn't even have time to take my coat off before I collapsed inside the door and wept as I have never wept in my whole life. She tried to get me to talk, but I was sobbing so hard that I had to gasp for breath, and the sound coming out of my throat was a high-pitched tone that I didn't recognize and that wouldn't stop. I don't know how long I huddled there, half lying, half sitting on the floor, held tight in her arms but unable to calm myself. She asked repeatedly what the matter was, but I could hardly get a word out, it took forever for me to utter the one sentence, the sentence that said the way things were: She's lost. She got me a cognac and hauled me into a chair. You have no idea, Renate, I whispered over and over, nobody could have an idea about what a monster the man is. He doesn't love her, he doesn't need her, he doesn't even desire her, I'm sure of that. But then what does he want with her? asked Renate, still baffled. He's training her, I said, he's turning her into an animal, he keeps her like an animal, he's made her completely obedient, and that's all that interests him. It's much worse than you can imagine, he's really untouched by any sexual feeling, I could sense that, he's untouched by anything, he just wants to have power over her and I think he's succeeded. He didn't show a trace of anxiety, he's utterly without scruple, he can rely on Daniela. He's achieved it, I could see that; she's like his slave, she's lost.

Of course I still tried to talk to Daniela one more time. Renate had given me the courage to try, but it was advice from someone who was clueless; she hadn't seen him or spoken to him. I picked Daniela up when she came out of school; I had taken the time off and was having an outing with her, because I didn't want Irmi to feel there was something that had to be hidden from her. She sat beside me in silence, her eyes scrunched closed against the wind as we drove, and shrugged when I asked her where should we go. It doesn't matter where you read me your sermon, Mama, she said in the biting, ironic way that she had mastered recently. The less far we go, the sooner it'll be over. But I drove to the Upper Forest, from where you can go on the most wonderful walks; I even said something about eating ice cream and immediately knew I was being absurd; we were here precisely because there wasn't an ice cream in the world that gave Daniela pleasure anymore, even if she was as thin as a child as she sat perched there next to me. I parked the car by the edge of the forest where the paths began; we walked once around the lake and I tried everything. I didn't make any reproaches and I didn't preach at her either, but I even finally described my visit, the coldness this man exuded, the absolute lack of interest in her as a person that I had sensed, the cynical way he talked. I was boring her. I couldn't reach her. It didn't interest her. She didn't tell me a thing about herself or about him, she listened apathetically to what I had to say, and now and again she hit the trees with a dry stick, like a boy. She was wearing jeans and a dark blue sweater and looked fifteen, except that there was nothing childlike left in her eyes. You know, Mama, she said when we were in the car again, I think you're jealous. And not once did she look at me.

■ ■ ■

Today she went to headquarters. Early in the morning there was a call saying that the appointment had to be put back an hour, otherwise I would never have known about it. I came home from work earlier than usual, hoping she might tell me about it, but she sat silent at the supper table, her eyes still red from crying, and slowly stirred a spoon around in her tea. Ernst was at a club rehearsal, and Irmi went to bed early, so I did the dishes and then sat in the kitchen with no idea what to do, while she made noises in the bath upstairs. She had always liked being in water; when she was a child, we had sometimes taken baths together and she had squawked with joy when a plastic duck or a frog came swimming toward her.

■ ■ ■

After our walk at the lake, I tried to talk to Ernst. I didn't tell him anything about the scene in the bar, I said I had seen the two of them in an ice cream place. I told him that Daniela hadn't been coming home at night for a long time now, but came tiptoeing up the stairs in her stocking feet shortly before breakfast. I told him that I had tracked down this Willrodt person at home. I didn't tell him things that I felt but couldn't prove. I let things rest with what was provable, and already bad enough. But he didn't believe me. If a girl of seventeen goes to eat ice cream with a man in broad daylight, it's no cause to spy on her, he said. As for my capacity to judge men, the change in my own life spoke for itself. He was quite aware of what time his daughter came home. Besides that he had had a long conversation with Daniela only recently, she had told him about her plans to study, asked about her savings account, and had behaved perfectly sensibly. There could be no question that the child needed help, and if she did, she certainly didn't need it from her mother.

My restlessness came back. I had kept myself quite well under control of late, but since my conversation with Willrodt, my nerves were worn thin. Sometimes I had a feeling that there was sandpaper inside my eyelids, and my forehead ached. Even when I drank absolutely nothing in the evening, I found it harder to pull myself together next morning. I was always hunting for something; mostly it was my keys, then it was my glasses, which I'd had to wear for some years now, then it was my wallet. My purse had become my enemy, I was always scrabbling around in its black leather depths for whatever was needed at that moment. My impatience was a burden even to myself, I found even waiting in line when doing my shopping unbearable. I looked into the faces of other men with suspicion, and wondered if they were capable of the same acts as Willrodt. I kept misreading things in a macabre way, I saw "tumor" instead of "humor," "death" instead of "breath," "pet" instead of "wet." Daniela watched me with a kind of indulgent distaste; she believed I was concerned about her, but she found it overtly funny. She didn't change her lifestyle in any way whatsoever; she still came home around dawn, she still went to school and did her homework, Irmi was still oblivious, and Ernst still looked in the other direction. She was cunning enough to be particularly vigilant with him, and every evening she had a new, harmless reason for going out: preparing for a class test, going to a movie, meeting friends in an ice cream parlor, a birthday party for a girl in her class. She wore jeans when she went out and apparently came back in jeans as well; what she had on her body in the meantime—if anything at all—I could only imagine. Willrodt never telephoned and never made any kind of appearance; if I hadn't seen the two of them in the bar that time, I would still have had absolutely no idea what was going on. And then one morning I spotted the marks on her neck. Daniela noticed me looking at her at the breakfast table; the velvet kerchief she wore had slipped, and she saw my horrified face as she was reaching for the coffeepot, and she quickly pulled it back into place. At first I thought they were hickeys—that's what they were called when I was young—but they were too small for that; there also seemed to be several of them, at almost regular intervals. Our eyes met and for the first time I saw that something was different. She was off-balance, she didn't grin once, she herself seemed a bit frightened as she sensed my distress, a bit embarrassed or confused. I tried to stop her in the doorway; she already had her anorak on and her schoolbag in her hand. Perhaps I pressed too hard in my panic and relief that she wasn't rebuffing all contact; anyhow she slipped past me, murmuring that everything was fine, and almost threw herself out of the house. I let the door swing back closed and began to hunt up my things—as always in those days a tormenting business that involved going through almost every room. I got into the car. My thoughts were racing and I also felt very ill. I tried to think what Ernst could do if only he finally believed me. L. was small, too small for someone like Willrodt to carry on his excesses once more people knew. Ernst belonged to almost every club and organization in the town; he bowled with men from the security forces, in our chorus there were members of the police, even a public prosecutor. Even Willrodt had only rented his discos and semi-bordellos; the buildings must belong to someone, someone granted the licenses and someone could also organize a police raid now and then. It should certainly be possible to spoil his business a little or at least make it harder and thus take away his pleasure in his little games. Someone like Willrodt didn't reach for little girls who were still learning their Latin vocabulary, he kept his hands off daughters of middle-class families if it was too dangerous for him. Maybe it was a particular pleasure for him that he now had such a girl at his disposal, who was still totally unspoiled when she fell into his hands, who took ballet lessons and could play the piano and didn't come out of the filth like him and everyone he knew. But knowing all this didn't help; I had no influence with Ernst anymore.

A young girl ran out in front of the car. I braked so hard that the tires screamed the way they do in a crime series on TV, and I clutched the steering wheel as if my life depended on it. She had stopped dead and was looking right at me, saw the horror on my face, and that was when the fright suddenly hit her, I think. She had set out across the street, assuming I had seen her—I must have been a long way away, I'm sure I was driving far too fast. I hadn't noticed the light, and I hadn't registered the young girl at all. I could have run right over her; she was about the same age as Daniela.

That was when I first had the idea, and then it wouldn't go away. I drove the car along the side of the road, my whole body shaking. The girl had gone on; she didn't even seem angry, perhaps she hadn't felt any fear herself, only recognized mine. I saw myself gray-faced in the rearview mirror, I looked absolutely wiped out and at least ten years older than I really was. It was only a tiny thing, maybe going five miles over the limit, a half minute lost in thought or just enough time to light a cigarette. The situation unrolled in such a minuscule lapse of time that it was almost impossible to measure, and the causes could be so insignificant, so foolishly infinitesimal. It would have been an accident.

And that's what it was. It was almost two months later when Renate called me in the office to say she was coming for an afternoon. We agreed to meet at Hirmer's pastry shop, because it was easy to stroll from there, although we both knew that there would be no strolling.

So I did the shopping beforehand and when I reached our café, she was already installed in our favorite spot, in the corner on the sofa. She had lots to tell me about her real estate agent; they were looking for a new apartment, they'd taken a vacation in America, he worshiped the ground she walked on, he was a total gentleman, as solid as ever, but not sad anymore. She looked better than ever and was strikingly dressed and made up, which looked good on her. She showed me photos from M. and New York and talked about their beginnings in the brokerage business; it could have been a wonderful afternoon. She saw that I was feeling very down, but she didn't ask why; perhaps she didn't want to hear the old stories again, but I think it more likely that she didn't want to make me even sadder. When we were having our farewell sherry I was on the verge of tears, but that's when she had to go to the ladies' room, and nothing came of it. Otherwise we'd certainly have stayed longer.

　　　　■ ■ ■

The street was empty and it was drizzling a little, as it often did in this region. The twilight was giving way to darkness—so you can't say that visibility was good. Perhaps that's why I was so late in spotting him, but it was also probably because I was deep in thought. There he stood on the street, right under the streetlight, in a tight-fitting raincoat with his hands in his pockets and his head pulled in against the wet; a light was shining on him from behind, so I saw the beak of a nose, and the dark hair plastered to his head. He was all alone, there was no one else on the street, and no one on a bicycle; no neighborhood to be going for a walk, so close to the industrial area, no shops, no trees for dogs. I could have decided otherwise. All I had to do was stop, stand still, do nothing, and the moment would have been gone. But it was the moment I had been waiting for since I first got to know him; it was a gift of a moment, like luck, something that couldn't be induced or artificially created, an extraordinary chance, something that is called fate when it really appears to one, and it really appeared to me. In that fraction of a second when I saw him standing there and was already slowing the car, it all went racing through my head—all that, and what I'd already thought before and all the previous weeks and months; they say that a dying man sees his whole life once more like a wildly speeded up film; that's how it was for me too, but I wasn't the one to die, he was. I put my foot on the gas just as he started to walk and I pushed the car up to very high speed very quickly; I had always driven fast cars, for pleasure, and now that pleasure was also being put to use. I drove at him, he didn't even look round, maybe he was deep in thought. I got him from the side. That's how it was.

A NOTE ON THE TYPE

The text of this book was set in Sabon, a typeface designed by Jan Tschichold (1902–1974), the well-known German typographer. Based loosely on the original designs by Claude Garamond (c. 1480–1561), Sabon is unique in that it was explicitly designed for hotmetal composition on both the Monotype and Linotype machines as well as for filmsetting. Designed in 1966 in Frankfurt, Sabon was named for the famous Lyons punch cutter Jacques Sabon, who is thought to have brought some of Garamond's matrices to Frankfurt.

Composed by Creative Graphics, Inc.,
Allentown, Pennsylvania

Printed and bound by R. R. Donnelley & Sons
Harrisonburg, Virginia

Designed by Soonyoung Kwon